To Gene
With all best
wishes. And in
with the writing!
Best,
Jim Richards

LOVE BENEATH THE NAPALM

The *Notre Dame Review* Book Prize

LOVE

beneath the

NAPALM

Stories

James D. Redwood (signature)

JAMES D. REDWOOD

University of Notre Dame Press
Notre Dame, Indiana

Published by the University of Notre Dame Press
Notre Dame, Indiana 46556
www.undpress.nd.edu

Library of Congress Cataloging-in-Publication Data

Redwood, James D., 1949–
    [Short stories. Selections]
    Love beneath the napalm : stories / James D. Redwood.
        pages   cm
    "The Notre Dame Review Book Prize."
    ISBN-13: 978-0-268-04034-5 (pbk. : alk. paper)
    ISBN-10: 0-268-04034-6 (pbk. : alk. paper)
    1. Vietnam War, 1961–1975—Psychological aspects—Fiction.
I. Title.
    PS3618.E43537A6 2013
    813'.6—dc23
                                                2013022752

∞ *The paper in this book meets the guidelines for permanence and durability of the Committee
on Production Guidelines for Book Longevity of the Council on Library Resources.*

This book is dedicated to the memory of the following:

DENNIS A. TROUTE
(1946–2012)

NBC (and later ABC) news reporter, Brodard and Givral's friend, who kindly gave me a place to stay after curfew on the night of December 2, 1973, when the North Vietnamese blew up the Nha Be oil storage depot and shattered the windows of his Saigon apartment thirteen miles away; and

Photo by Neal Ulevich

THE UNKNOWN GIRL WITH THE GUITAR
(195?–1970)

whose death compelled the story "The Photograph," and who, it is the hope of this author, has long since ceased to be a Wandering Soul and has found a lasting measure of peace.

Photo by Le Minh Truong

"No matter what happens, keep on living, Mamselle. A living human being is, after all, Nature's most beautiful creation."
　　　　　　　　　　　　　—Leonid Leonov, *The Thief*

contents

a c k n o w l e d g m e n t s

I would like, first and foremost, to thank my dear wife Dolly, for believing so tenaciously in me, and Melissa Paa Redwood and Daniel William Redwood, the best young people it has been my privilege to know.

I would also like to thank William O'Rourke, the wonderful editor of the *Notre Dame Review,* for believing so tenaciously in my writing, as well as all the truly superb people at the University of Notre Dame Press who have worked so hard to bring this project to fruition, including Elizabeth Sain, Wendy McMillen, Robyn Karkiewicz, Susan Berger, Kathryn Pitts, and Stephen Little. My deepest appreciation to each and every one of you.

And I would also like to thank the following individuals, in no particular order, for their kind help and encouragement along the way: David Lynn, Nancy Zafris, Sharon Dilworth, Robert Anderson, James Carl Nelson, the late Staige Blackford, Peter White, Christopher N. May, Norman R. Shapiro, my brother John Redwood III, David Pratt, and Alex Seita.

Because this book evolved out of my experiences in Southeast Asia in the early 1970s, I also wish to express my especial gratitude to Dick Hughes, Nguyen Thi Minh Ha, and Nguyen Thi Minh Phuong, without whose friendship I would know far less than I do about Viet Nam and its courageous people.

———

The following eight stories have been previously published:

"The Photograph" was published in *The Kenyon Review* (New Series) 26, no. 4 (Fall 2004): 85–97.

"The Stamp Collector" was published in *TriQuarterly* 125 (2006): 159–69.

"The Son Returns" was published in *Black Warrior Review* 26, no. 2 (Spring/Summer 2000): 166–78.

"The Black Phantom" was published in *North Dakota Quarterly* 72, no. 4 (Fall 2005): 120–30.

"Love Beneath the Napalm" was published in *Notre Dame Review*, no. 19 (Winter 2005): 13–23 ("And Then" section). It was reprinted in John Matthias and William O'Rourke, eds., *Notre Dame Review: The First Ten Years* (Notre Dame: University of Notre Dame Press, 2009): 428–38.

"Numbers" was published in *Virginia Quarterly Review* 75, no. 2 (Spring 1999): 385–96.

"Brother Daniel's Roses" was published in *Notre Dame Review*, no. 29 (Winter/Spring 2010): 44–54.

"The Summer Associate" was published in *Notre Dame Review*, no. 33 (Winter/Spring 2012): 42–52.

LOVE BENEATH THE NAPALM

one

THE PHOTOGRAPH

Nguyen Van Manh crept along the border of the Lake of the Restored Sword, where the magic tortoise dwelt. Ever since he'd arrived in Hanoi the night before, a city swept up in rejoicing over the end of the war, Manh had run across thousands of people, his fellow veterans mostly, dressed like him in drab olive uniforms and sweat-stained pith helmets with a red star in the middle, and all of them happy, celebrating, ecstatic as newborn stars in the unfamiliar firmament of peace. In 1428, at the completion of another war, Emperor Le Loi had returned the symbolic sword with which he'd defeated the Chinese to the huge tortoise and walked away from the lake in triumph, a hero beloved of his people for all time. First Class Private Manh, barely noticeable in his shabby fatigues, halted in front of a soup vendor dispensing steaming bowls of *pho* under a *sau* tree outside the Hoa Phong Tower.

"Excuse me," he said, his voice straining to make itself heard above the din of early morning trams and Moskwa automobiles carrying people to work. "Can you tell me where Comrade Photographer Ngo Khai Duong lives?"

Just as the words were out of his mouth, Manh noticed the customer into whose bowl the old merchant was ladling soup. The young woman, who was turned away from him, was also dressed in fatigues. A floppy field hat clung to her forehead, under which her straight black hair drooped down her back. Manh felt a strange tightening in his chest, as though he'd been dragged under the surface of Restored Sword Lake by the renowned turtle itself and could no longer breathe. From behind, the woman might have been mistaken for Mei-linh.

"What did you ask, young man?" the soup seller said, his ladle suspended above the girl's bowl. He glared suspiciously at the threadbare veteran in front of him. Vermicelli noodles wiggled like worms in the middle of the ladle.

Manh was terrified the young woman might turn around. *The dead do not return to earth to eat soup,* he told himself. But still he could not speak.

"Young man?" the vendor asked again, impatiently. He finished serving the girl, who wheeled at last.

"I was wondering where Ngo Khai Duong lives," Manh said, easily now, relieved at the woman's homeliness. Her face was squat and brown, like a potato, her nose flatter than most, her eyes set so far apart they looked as though they were trying to escape from each other. Smallpox scars pitted her face as well.

"Duong, the famous photographer," Manh repeated.

The vendor gazed at him through a wreath of mist which rose from the aluminum pot in which his *pho* brewed. The old man stirred the soup to keep it off the boil.

"What do you want with a man like *him?*" he asked. "Comrade Duong is being made a Councillor of State today, even while we speak. Our whole neighborhood is proud of it."

He sniffed in reflected glory at these last words and cast another disparaging look at the tattered PAVN private. The heroes who had saved the country in April 1975 were now the outcasts of May.

"For his photographs, you know," the old man went on. A customer called from the other side of the soup stand, and the seller pointedly turned his back on Manh and strode away.

"Indeed, they *are* marvelous, don't you think, Comrade?" the young woman slurping her soup whispered. "The photographs, I mean," she added nervously.

She spoke up too soon, too eagerly, and Manh ruthlessly turned his back on her the way the soup vendor had on him. *What right did she have to talk about these photographs?* He was suddenly resentful of her. *What right did she have to be sitting there at all?* He was about to tramp away when the old man turned back.

"Return after dark," he said. "Number 17, Liberation Court. Right over there."

He jerked his head toward a building across the street, then flitted once more to the far side of the soup cart. Manh spun on his heels and stalked off without a word to the young cadre who still sat patiently above her bowl, gazing at him. How *dare* she remind him of Mei-linh!

———

"Here, girl, let me show you."

Ngo Khai Duong cocked his squat black Hasselblad up onto his shoulder like a soldier hoisting his rifle to attention and strutted over to Mei-linh. His stringy salt-and-pepper hair was combed straight back over his temples in a rakish manner that reminded Manh of the playboy Emperor Bao Dai, and a Cambodian cigarette from which a long trail of ash hung down dangled from his mouth. He smacked his lips together as he came up to her, and his yellow, nicotine-stained teeth looked like a dog's preparing to bite. Manh winced with displeasure as he looked on. With his free hand the great photographer tugged Mei-linh by the shirt sleeve, first to the left, and then, when that was not satisfactory, he cupped his fingers around the ball of her shoulder and nudged her gently back to the right. Manh's eyes narrowed as he noticed how long Duong's hand lingered on Mei-linh's shoulder. Until, in fact, the girl blushed.

"There, that is good," the photographer said, his face melting into a smile as he stepped backward. He flicked the ash from his cigarette and then slipped it between his lips again. He gazed at Mei-linh appreciatively.

"You *are* a pretty bird, you know," he said. "Now sit on that rock and pretend to play that guitar of yours. But don't block the others," he chided. "They'll look good in the background. Out of focus, of course."

He chuckled, and with a toss of his hand indicated two rather plain-looking female soldiers seated on another rock directly behind Mei-linh, swiftly shoveling rice into their mouths from a couple of earthenware bowls. The lunch time for Detonation Squad Number 2 had been reduced to ten minutes after the American bombing picked up. Having caught the eye of Ngo Khai Duong, however, Mei-linh could eat later, and take as long as she liked.

"No, no, you don't actually have to *do* it," Duong said impatiently, when Mei-linh suddenly began to play her guitar, delicately, beautifully. Manh watched her, enchanted. Mei-linh played on and on, strumming her heart out, ignoring the black looks of the photographer and the protesting whirr of his camera. . . .

———

Manh wandered the streets with time to kill rather than an enemy. A force as irresistible as love impelled him in the direction of the Old Quarter, where he knew he would only be sad. He shuffled past laughing crowds of shoppers, eager to capitalize on the changes wrought by the Great Spring Victory, who shoved and jostled one another in high good spirits to get at the wonderful wares displayed in the hundreds of trade shops which had replaced the guilds of Le Loi's time. Watches, belts, hairpins, foreign cosmetics, lacquer boxes, silver and gold jewelry, reed mats, bamboo furniture. He stopped at a votive objects shop on Ma May and bought a sheaf of ghost paper, which he carried to a nondescript tube house on Hang Dao Street. His eyes welled up as he gazed at the tiny, glass-enclosed foyer where, before the war, Mei-linh and her mother had sold their red-dyed silk goods. The light glanced off the glass, and Manh saw a fleeting figure inside. His heart leaped so violently he felt it pounding in his throat, and he bounded forward and let out a muffled cry. A fat Indian moneylender glared back at him from the other side of the window, a mistrustful glint in his eye. Manh's hands trembled with disappointment as he took the votive paper from his pocket. The moneylender scowled at him as he lit it with a match, cupped his hands in a swift prayer, and then dropped the flaming fragments onto the sidewalk in front of the house. *Nor do the dead come back to sell the things of this world,* he thought mournfully, as he watched the paper burn.

"Get along with you, vagrant!" the Indian yelled, sticking his head through the door.

Manh turned away, his shoulders slumped as though he carried the entire sorrow of the war just ended all by himself. . . .

Late in the afternoon he became hungry and stopped for a plate of *cha xuong song* at an outdoor restaurant across from the central rail station. Three years earlier, he and Mei-linh had caught a troop train together from the same station, and his chest clamped up as he remembered it. The train was crowded with hundreds of ardent Youth Volunteers like themselves, their eyes glittering with revolutionary zeal, their hearts pounding a steady drumbeat to victory in the south.

Over the loudspeakers hanging from the station portico, Premier Pham Van Dong exhorted the country to forget the horrors of the war and move forward. Manh thought of Mei-linh again, and his jaw tightened. *Were those who'd lost so much to be forgotten, too?* His face muscles rippled with anger. *Who had the right to sacrifice her again?*

"My fellow citizens," the premier droned, "the day has finally arrived when our great country has thrown off the shackles of colonialism. Peace has come at last, and now we must focus on reform."

The blast of a train whistle drowned out the premier's next words, and Manh looked up from the restaurant as another troop load of veterans arrived from the south. Now that the stern work of the war was over, the commanders had allowed the men and women to mingle freely, and several of the male cadres laughed heartily, their arms around the women, and waved bottles of Chinese and Russian beer. Manh saw a young man wheel suddenly to the woman next to him and give her a long kiss. The girl burst into a giggle and slapped him playfully, but then stuck her cheek up to be kissed again. Manh turned his eyes away and stared sullenly at the last bit of pork on his plate. How different it had been when he and Mei-linh were prodded like cattle into separate cars the day they left, only to be reunited in the jungle two weeks later. There was no time then for kisses, for laughter. . . .

"It is time to move on, Comrades," Premier Dong intoned, his voice crackling with enthusiasm. "The war is over! Let us move forward with reform!"

Manh felt a sudden ache deep inside his stomach. He thrust his plate away and scowled at the repeated mantra of reform. The picture of Mei-linh lay before him in his mind, as sharp and clear as on the day Ngo Khai Duong had photographed her. Without her he felt like a man from whom the vital organs had been removed, a victim of the same explosion. What good was it to talk of reform?

"March with me!" Premier Dong concluded, his voice nearly hysterical now. "I command you! Forward!"

Manh scraped his chair back so vehemently it tipped over and clattered to the ground. The restaurant owner and several patrons stared at him, but he left the chair where it lay and stormed off. No one, not even the premier, had the right to order him to move on.

After taking his pictures Ngo Khai Duong reluctantly agreed to watch that day's performance, a rehashing of Le Loi's victory over the Chinese, meant to inspire the troops and give them the necessary will to go out and defuse the unexploded American bombs left behind after every air strike. The great photographer fidgeted in his field chair, however, muttering to Manh how anxious he was to develop his films and return to Hanoi.

"Recently the audience has been captivated more by the music than the acting," Manh said, hoping to spark his interest. How proud he was to say it, too! His soul stirred with admiration for Mei-linh.

"Really?" Duong said, yawning. He shrugged and glanced down at his Rolex, then stared off into space. Manh was miffed at the man's indifference and pulled back from him. His temples were throbbing wildly now, as they did every time right before the musicians stepped onstage. Eagerly he craned his neck as they filed in at last, in strict order of precedence. Bung, the bamboo flautist, Vu with his violin, Huynh the *dan tranh* zither player, and finally Mei-linh with her guitar slung over her shoulder. Manh caught his breath when for some reason the others suddenly stepped aside, like abashed moons retreating at dawn, and allowed Mei-linh to seat herself at the very front of the stage. His heart warmed with gratitude at this unexpected acknowledgment of her superiority. He glanced joyfully at the man beside him. Ngo Khai Duong was yawning again. Manh's fingers twitched with annoyance. How he longed to throttle him!

Just then Mei-linh set her jaw with determination and began to play, and the chords of a melody divine enough to enslave the Emperor of Jade himself floated out over the enraptured audience. The great photographer looked at the stage for the first time. Suddenly he sat bolt upright, and his eyes sparkled with interest.

"Beautiful," he murmured fervently. "Simply beautiful!"

Manh peeked at him, pleased.

"Yes," he said proudly. "Isn't her playing *magnificent?*"

———

He lingered at the edge of the Lake of the Restored Sword and watched the sun set. The purple blossoms of the *loc vung* trees glittered gaily in the fading light, but their loveliness failed to cheer him. The soup vendor outside the Hoa Phong Tower had already closed up his shop and departed for the night. In the distance Manh heard the jubilant sounds of party bands at the Museum of the Revolution, loudly playing the carefree songs of liberation, most of them French or American. Their upbeat tones filled him with deep sadness.

It grew dark, and young couples started to converge on the lake, some of them boldly holding hands just like westerners, proudly showing off their eagerness to move on. The slow strumming of a guitar came from across the water, which was the color of black silk in the brief hour of the unrisen moon. Nguyen Van Manh flinched at the sound, then sighed.

"Why are you not celebrating the victory, Comrade?"

In the darkness the young woman reminded him of Mei-linh from the front now, and he tensed as she approached. She had a thick book in her hand, the place marked with her fore-finger, and Manh suspected she'd spent the day at the Temple of Literature. He itched to drag her into the lighted street where her ugliness would console him. The feeling troubled him.

"Have you been waiting for me . . . , Comrade?" he asked.

She laughed lightly, like a spoon clinking against a glass rim, and Manh found himself wishing the laugh had been coarser, more appropriate for a woman with a face like hers.

"Hardly. Like yourself, I am waiting for the return of Councillor Duong." She nodded in the direction of the photographer's apartment. At that moment an explosion shattered the relative stillness of the night, and a brilliant flash of color lit up the sky. Manh knew there'd be fireworks, but nevertheless he shrank into a defensive posture as though they might obliterate him.

More explosions came, more flashes of light. Had Premier Dong gone back on his word? The girl laughed merrily again.

"Relax, Comrade. The festivities are ending. Photographer Duong will be coming back soon."

Manh gathered heart from the increasing light. Fireworks erupted all around them now. Then the moon rose, and a pale orange disc smiled on the waters of the Lake of the Restored Sword. Suddenly he was hit with a sharp pang, however.

"I'm sorry I was so . . . rude to you this morning," he said. In the light of a particularly large explosion he noticed an unoccupied bench on the edge of the lake. He indicated it with his hand. "Would you like to sit down?"

She nodded, and they moved slowly toward it. On the bench next to them nuzzled a couple of lovers, the girl's head cocked against the man's shoulder. They whispered to each other, their voices as sweet as the murmur of wind through grass. As he looked at them, Manh felt his loss more intensely than at any other time since he'd arrived in the capital, and it pained him like the probing of a knife which had found his heart at last. The young veteran girl sat down beside him, and he felt a sudden yearning for her, as though she might be able to remove the knife without hurting him. The yearning was accompanied by a strange, sad tenderness.

She turned to watch the couple snuggling on their bench, and the sight of her floppy field hat and her long black hair glistening in the moonlight reminded him of how he'd first come to notice her that morning. He felt like a man caught on the brink of infidelity, and he drew his breath in sharply to cleanse himself of guilt. His resentment for her returned. What a temptress she was, coming on to him like that! And yet how slatternly she was! Just then she turned back to him, and the smile on her face faded instantly at the frown on Manh's. She trembled, the lines etched into her potato face indicating her distress, and Manh's annoyance at her instantly evaporated.

"I'm sorry," he said again, making his tone as gentle as he could.

She laughed a third time, but the lightness was gone now.

"Oh, it's all right," she said, hesitantly. "I sensed you had an important reason for seeing Photographer Duong. You were very serious."

Manh gazed toward the Lake of the Restored Sword while the happy couple continued to warble next to them. His eye caught the tall granite statue of Le Loi, meant to last the ages, astride his pedestal, the magic sword clutched triumphantly in his hand. Some cheerful young tourists, too young to be drafted, stared up at it in admiration. Manh clenched his jaws. Did any of them have any idea just how many bones it took to build a monument to a great war hero? Or whose they were? He tore his glance away from the adoring little group, afraid of what he might do if he didn't.

"Am I correct?" his companion asked timidly.

He bit his lip and swallowed hard, then looked away again, this time toward Writing Brush Tower and the Sunbeam Bridge on the other side of the lake. The nagging ache knotted up his stomach again. Of course he had an important reason for seeing such a man! Yet how could he explain it to *her*?

He'd begged Mei-linh not to join the patrol sent out to defuse the remaining bombs after Ngo Khai Duong's driver accidentally stepped on one lurking in the Lao grass like a krait. She was still shaking from her meeting with the great photographer, just after the performance, in the darkened tent where he did his developing work. Duong's high-handedness must have offended her greatly, for she'd left the photograph behind her in the tent. But she didn't want to talk about it and instead stalked off on the heels of the detonation squad. Manh followed her with his eyes, hoping she might relent, but then he turned sadly away when she did not. . . .

"And you?" he asked. "Why do *you* wish to see Photographer Duong?"

The young woman squirmed in her seat.

"My mother sent me," she said softly. "She wishes me to get a photograph from him, if I can."

Manh leaned instinctively toward her, then suddenly backed off.

"That is what I want, too. How strange!"

Tears glistened in her eyes, and she glanced down at her feet.

"You see, Photographer Duong snuck into Quang Tri right before the puppet troops retook it during our great Easter offensive," she said. "My brother and a squad of four other men were left behind to keep our flag flying over the citadel. Ngo Khai Duong snapped some pictures of them and got out barely in time. One of the photos later appeared in an issue of *Viet-Nam Pictorial,* and my mother saw it by chance. She cried over it for days. Now she has sent me to see if Comrade Duong has any others which she can keep for herself. She no longer wants to share him with the rest of the world."

Manh listened carefully. His heart beat in sympathy at her loss, but then the image of Mei-linh playing her guitar crept into his mind and knocked the young woman's brother off the ramparts of the Quang Tri Citadel. Slowly he drew away from her. He, too, was tired of sharing Mei-linh—with Ngo Khai Duong.

They climbed the one short flight of stairs together, but by then the girl, who introduced herself as Tran Thi Trinh, had recovered her composure. Manh was struck with the elegant wrought-iron banister, the beautiful chandelier which hung over the staircase like a huge ice crystal, the carved moldings and sculpted plasterwork. Their boots tramped noisily across the translucent marble floor, which reflected back in Manh's face the new opulence which was the shape of things to come, at least for those lucky enough to be in the vanguard of reform. The house had once belonged to the Assistant Governor General of Tonkin and was now rented out to several stars of the revolution. Manh knocked loudly on the mahogany door several times, afraid the sound might not penetrate the rich thick wood.

The door creaked open, and a man dressed in an ill-fitting black tuxedo and stocky as a seladang bull stood before them, weaving from side to side. His hair was all gray now, his nose as red as an overripe jambu, and broken capillaries stood out on both cheeks like purple spider webs. Manh leaned back as he caught a whiff of the man's breath. Good living had aged the great photographer considerably in the last three years.

"Comrade Duong?" the veteran asked, irritated at the trepidation in his voice. "We'd like to speak with you, please."

"It's *Councillor* Duong," the man said self-importantly, puffing his chest out so that his medals sparkled in the light of the chandelier which hung from the ceiling, the twin of the one outside. He staggered forward and squinted at the figure cringing behind Nguyen Van Manh.

"Well, hello, who's this?" he said unctuously, steadying himself against Manh's shoulder. His half-full champagne glass bobbed in his hand as he tried to stay upright, and some of the wine splashed across Manh's chest, which was not decorated with medals. Manh made a face and shook the liquid off.

"Why, you're a nice one!" Duong exclaimed to Trinh, running his eyes up and down her body. "Come in! Come in! You know, you two are my first official petitioners! Think of that! What do you want, anyway?"

He offered his arm to Trinh, but she shrank even further behind her companion. Ngo Khai Duong's eyes glittered fiercely at her, panther-like, but he merely shrugged and looped his arm through Manh's instead.

"Let's go into the parlor," he said, twisting round and dragging Manh after him. "Houseboy!" he cried, at the top of his lungs. "More champagne!"

Manh immediately spotted the photograph among a number of others on a table by the fireplace. But just as Mei-linh had taken precedence at the performance in the jungle, so too her picture did now. It stood in a large gilt frame at the front of the table. Manh caught his breath and stared at it. His temples pulsed violently as he approached it, like a suppliant to an altar, and it was as though he was facing the living Mei-linh again.

Photographer Duong had gotten the light just right. It shone full on the left side of her body, accentuating the beautiful lines of her face, the silken smoothness of her skin, the velvet luxuriance of her hair, which hung down over her shoulder to below the fret of the guitar. The right half, down to the hand which delicately strummed the strings and which glittered in the sunlight like the fingers of Calliope, lay in the shadow and gave an exquisite chiaroscuro effect to the entire photograph. Manh's heart churned over and over as he studied it. He was in the presence of a masterpiece! He lowered his gaze, as if in prayer, and the sea-green tiles on the parlor floor began to glisten as his eyes filled. Then his sight cleared, and he glanced up again, his soul overflowing. Behind him he heard a series of short nervous laughs and suddenly remembered he was not alone. How could he have failed to appreciate the creator of such a divine work? He was ashamed of himself, and felt a sudden rush of affection for Ngo Khai Duong for having prized her so greatly. But he *had* to have the photograph.

"Councillor Duong," he said respectfully, turning around. "I was wondering whether—"

He stopped in amazement when he saw the photographer's hand move up and down Cadre Trinh's thigh, stroking it gently. The girl sat frozen in horror. As the hand went higher, she fidgeted and let out a gasp. Manh felt extremely embarrassed. A white-frocked servant scurried up to the sofa with three champagne glasses tinkling on a salver. Tran Thi Trinh desperately shook her head, but Ngo Khai Duong quickly swept up both their glasses with his free hand and pulled them to him. He tossed one off, then started on the other. The houseboy came over to Manh, who angrily shook him off. He did not know why he was angry. He continued to stare open-mouthed at the couple on the sofa.

"You can have any one you like, my dear," Duong was saying, tapping a photo album with his finger. "I am pleased to help out your dear old mother. But there is something you can also do for *me*."

He winked insinuatingly at her, and she emitted a loud unnatural laugh like a sparrow screeching in a cactus hedge. She darted her eyes to the floor. Then she tried to pull back from him, but his hand was firmly cupped around her upper thigh, the way Manh had once seen it on Mei-linh's shoulder, and she trembled in shame and continued to stare at the floor. Manh suddenly realized why he was so angry. He sprang forward.

"Comrade Duong!" he said sharply, and the old man started and spilled his champagne again. He set his glass down with a smack and scowled at Manh. Instinctively he kept his other hand on Cadre Trinh's thigh, however.

"You still here!" he exclaimed. "What do you want?"

Manh lurched to a halt as though the great photographer's question had broken his stride. He stared at the girl cowering at Ngo Khai Duong's side, then at the monument to the one who'd been past saving for years. Looking troubled, his eyes went back and forth, several times, until all of a sudden his brow cleared and his anger fell from him like a suit of clothes tumbling to the floor.

"This," he said firmly, picking up the photograph.

Duong gave it barely a glance. He burst into a short laugh and waved him away.

"Take it and go," he said impatiently, his other hand groping the girl again. "I have no use for *that* thing anymore."

He turned back to Trinh, baring his teeth like a jackal. The girl looked pleadingly at Manh, her hands clasped helplessly in front of her. She gulped like a terrified animal, several times, and her eyes shot wider apart each time she did so. Manh's fury at Ngo Khai Duong rose inside him again. He felt a brief stab of pity for the girl, but then an immense revulsion swept over him when her nostrils quivered anxiously and the blotches on her face turned a muddy, unsightly brown, like the run-off from a foul winter rain. He turned his rage on her with the swiftness of an explosion. Her ugliness was as indestructible as granite, and suddenly it exasperated him beyond measure. In a flash he set the picture down, bunched his fists, and advanced on her, seized with the urge to grab her by the throat and pound her face until it was beautiful, unrecognizable, capable of dying. She cried out in alarm when she saw him, and the feeling passed, but this time the pity died out of him as well. He stared stonily at the two of them, his eyes filled with equal hatred for them both. He clasped the photograph of Mei-linh to his chest.

Ngo Khai Duong watched him steadily. His lips slowly parted in a thin, humorless smile.

"My houseboy will see you out."

two

THE STAMP COLLECTOR

Phan Van Toan glued his eyes to the TV set above the soda cooler. The Marine assault on Grenada had just begun, and grainy pictures of C-130 Hercules transport planes and helicopters swooping down on the Pt. Salinas airfield flashed across the screen. He poured a fresh pot of water into the coffee machine and flipped the brew switch, as though giving a green light to the invasion. Hundreds of parachutists descended on the tarmac and fanned out in all directions as the odor of Hawaiian Kona filled the 7-Eleven shop. Toan's heart swelled with pride. He'd practically forgotten the humiliating suicide attack in Lebanon two days before, when 241 Marines had died in their barracks without even waking. The store clerk picked up the little American flag next to the cash register and twirled it back and forth. A satisfied smile spread across his lips. He'd just gotten his citizenship a month earlier.

A customer entered the shop. "Excuse me, you're Vietnamese, aren't you?" the man abruptly asked.

Toan reddened slightly and gazed at the American who stood across from him on the other side of the counter. He was about his own age, with gray flecks in his balding hair, and his face was cracked and weather-beaten. A stubby goatee hugged his chin like a tuft of vegetation on the face of a big rock. Toan winced at the smell of his sweat, which overpowered the scent of the Pine-Sol he'd applied to the floor tiles just before opening. The Southern California summer had stretched well into autumn, and every time someone entered the convenience store it was like yanking open the door of an oven. The man was dressed in a tattered U.S. Army jacket, and Toan suspected he was one of those unhappy veterans who drifted from place to place trying to escape their memories of the war. *His* war.

"Yes," Toan reluctantly admitted, his voice barely audible above the racket caused by the landing planes and helicopters. "I help you?"

The man nodded and reached into the pocket of his oil-stained jeans. He pulled out a letter and shoved it face up across the counter.

"I hope so," the American said. "I'd like you to translate this. I can pay."

He didn't look as though he had any money, but Toan picked the letter up nonetheless and read it at random. *Thuong anh.* A love letter. *Darling, I will be true to you forever. . . .* The paper was yellow, old, and brittle. The ink was of very poor quality, and had almost faded in spots. A North Vietnamese love letter.

"Where you get?" he asked.

The American glanced down at his feet, then up again. The hollows of his cheeks caved in as though he had trouble breathing.

"I got it off a man I killed. VC. I've had it for a long time, and—"

Just then the bell jangled above the door, and two boys in their early teens dashed into the 7-Eleven. Phan Van Toan's face darkened. The boys were riding skateboards, and the smaller one, Vi, Toan's nephew, had a Dodgers baseball cap reversed on his head. They popped in and out of the brightly-lit aisles stuffed with canned goods, snacks, and toiletries, skirted the bakery display and the ice cream freezer, and had almost made it to the magazine racks when Toan grabbed Vi's arm.

"You bad boy. No skateboard here! You know. *Di ve. Hieu khong?* Go home!"

The boy wiggled out of Toan's grasp and squared off in front of him. He jacked his skateboard up onto his arm. His friend kept going.

"It's a free country, Uncle! Remember? The U.S. of A!"

Toan lunged for him again, but Vi ducked behind a potato chip rack.

"Bad boy, I say. Your mother no like."

"*Your mother no like,*" Vi teased, from the safety of his shelter. "*Doesn't,* Uncle. Or *won't.*"

Toan's face went hot with embarrassment. Out of the corner of his eye, he spotted the other boy, Jimmy, stretching on tiptoes toward the top shelf of the magazine section, where the shopkeeper kept the shrink-wrapped *Playboy*s and *Penthouse*s. Toan bounded toward him, waving his arms about.

"You you!" he shouted. "No touch! Go home now."

The American teenager sank back down on his feet. Hurriedly he began thumbing through the latest issue of *Analog*. He looked as though he was just waiting for Toan to move away. All of a sudden the store clerk heard a crunch behind him.

"Pretty good, Uncle Toan. How much are they?"

Vi had helped himself to a small bag of Lay's. Toan's face blackened even further. But then he remembered the man with the letter, who waited patiently by the counter. Toan rushed up to him and bowed several times.

"I sorry," he said, taking care to keep one eye on Vi and his friend, however. "These boys, very bad." He shook his head.

The American peered at him. "That's okay. But will you translate the letter?"

Another assault group had landed at Pearls and was encountering some surprisingly tough resistance from a Cuban auxiliary force. The voice of the reporter accompanying them bristled with tension, but he was confident that opposition to the lightning advance would soon be crushed. Phan Van Toan glowed with pride again.

"I do for you tonight," he said, taking the letter and putting it in his pocket. Vi sprinted up to the counter, his mouth stained with potato chip grease. Toan glared at him, fished two quarters out of his pocket, opened the cash register, and dropped them inside. Then he slammed the register shut.

"You go now," he said sternly. "You lucky I no call your mother."

"It's a free country, Uncle," Vi repeated. He shrugged and turned away. "Hey, Jimmy! C'mon, we're outta here!" He plunked down his skateboard and jumped on. The other boy followed him out the door.

The American tapped Toan lightly on the sleeve. The shopkeeper looked at him.

"Thanks," the man said. "I'll be back tomorrow."

———

He'd gotten the itch back in Saigon, where he worked as Assessor to the Ministry of Ethnic Cultures. One day he was assigned to catalogue the Ministry's collection of stamps commemorating various minorities spread throughout the Central Highlands, and even farther north, in the land of the Communists. How lovely the images were, Toan thought, as he scrutinized the four of them under the lens of a high-powered microscope in the Ministry basement. Tiny arrows of desire, like the weapons of the Rhade tribe, began to shoot through him as he took the stamps, preserved on moisture-proof slides, and reluctantly locked them away in a fireproof safe. As he trudged up the stairs and out into the light, his heart burned with longing.

He started his own collection with the 12 xu stamp of the Tay, followed by the 10 xu H'mong and then the 12 xu Thai. All of these he found easily, after work, for a modest price at the public auction at the Museum of Fine Arts on Pho Duc Chinh Street. But the priceless 2 xu E de stamp, although ironically the cheapest in face value, eluded him like a beautiful woman, and he searched for it in vain, for months at a time, until he began to lose sleep over it and came to work exhausted and demoralized, with bags under his eyes. . . . Then one fateful evening, when he was alone at work, he took the Ministry's E de stamp and blamed it on the custodian, a Malay who was fired the next day. Toan's conscience bothered him for a while, but then his complete collection of ethnic minority stamps, which lay beneath his pillow in its own moisture-proof sheaf of anodized steel, although hard and cold to the touch, soothed him like a plush down comforter. The Malays, after all, were renowned for their thievery. . . .

———

Phan Van Toan brewed himself a cup of arrowroot tea and sat down at his living room table. The stench of fish sauce and cooking oil hung over his little apartment, a walk-up at the back of a three-story red brick building on the corner of Kenwood and Broadway, a block from the convenience store. The building had been a boardinghouse back in the thirties, and a subsequent owner had tried to spruce it up by adding wall-to-wall carpeting, wainscoting, and even some bas-relief cherubs to the trim above the kitchen cabinets. But the paint was cracked and peeling in places, and the plumbing on the floor above gurgled loudly through the pipes as Toan stirred his tea and gazed at the American's letter. With his knee he gently shoved his cot further under the table so he would have more room to work. His sister-in-law Mai, Khach's widow, told him he didn't have to worry about mortars and rockets anymore. But Phan Van Toan still slept under the table every night, his stamp collection beneath his pillow.

He stared at the yellowing parchment and picked up a pen. He took a sip of tea, stirred it again, took another sip, then stirred it a third time. He raised the gooseneck lamp beside the letter as high as it would go, decided the light was too dim, and lowered it until it hovered right over the page. The words that leaped out at him were all calculated to dismay him. *Love,* of course, the main one, but also *loyalty, trust, constancy.* . . . He wondered how long it had taken the young woman who'd written them to realize the futility of such fine sentiments, once they were stacked up against the hand fate had dealt her. His eyes drifted to the altar in the corner, where pictures of the family dead should have been. A knock sounded on the door.

Toan set down his pen and placed the lamp over the love letter. A second knock came, a more insistent one this time, and a cloud crossed his brow. He sprang up, checked to see that the room was in order, and strode to the door, smoothing the creases out of his trousers as he did so. He unlocked the door and swung it open. Mai stood before him, a folded-up dollar bill in her hand. She held it out to him.

"I'm sorry, Toan *oi,*" she said, placing the bill in his palm. "I've told that boy not to take advantage of you like that, but he just won't listen. I don't know what to do with him. May I come in?"

Toan had blocked the doorway and was trying to give the dollar back to her, but he stepped aside and let her enter. Mai worked in a garden shop on North Cedar Street, and the smell of fresh juniper blossoms filled the room as she gently brushed his hand away.

"No, keep it. I—" She gazed at the altar, and her eyes misted up. "Oh, Toan. I know you feel his loss so, but don't you think it's time? I could give you one of my photos, you know, and . . ."

Toan's face turned pale, and she let her offer trail off into the air. She pressed his hand.

"Are you sure you won't move in with us? It would be the best thing for Vi. He needs the firm grip of a man, and even though he makes fun of you, I know he loves you. He's just so *wild* sometimes." She shook her head.

Toan tried to return the dollar again, but it was moist with his sweat now and he laid it on the table instead.

"No, *chi* Mai," he said. His voice sounded curt, ungrateful, and he made an effort to take the edge off it. "Thanks," he added, softly. He returned the pressure of her hand, hoping she wouldn't notice how badly he was perspiring. "But I think I'd better stay here. It's quiet, you know, and—"

"I know," she interrupted, smiling sadly. "You realize that no one can replace . . . *him*"—again she looked at the vacant place on the altar—"in the eyes of his child. Not even his brother."

A sharp, stabbing pain shot through his frame, like the arrows of the Rhade again. He couldn't bear to look at her. Again she squeezed his hand.

"I love you for feeling it so," she said, and let out a sigh. Tears filled her eyes. "You miss him almost as much as I do, don't you?"

He let the question remain unanswered, and his gaze darted involuntarily to the love letter peeping out from the base of the lamp.

"What's that?" Mai asked, straining her eyes. Toan picked it up, but his hands were shaking so much he passed it off to her without a word.

"My!" she exclaimed. "A love letter! Where did you get *this?*" She gave him an arch look.

Toan forced a wan smile to his lips.

"It's not mine. An American came into the store today and asked me to translate it. So I said I would. Tonight."

Mai flashed him another sad smile.

"Oh, brother-in-law, you should find yourself a good woman here. It's been eight years, after all. I . . ."

She set the letter down on the table. Her glance returned to the altar.

"I will remain true to his memory, of course, but with *you* . . . it's different."

She eagerly scanned his face, and Toan struggled to retain his composure. He could no longer trust himself to speak.

"Thanks," she whispered, and pressed his hand one last time. "Thanks for remaining true to him as well."

———

While he waited for the American the next afternoon, Phan Van Toan gazed at the TV again, but his enthusiasm for the new war had faded. Cocky GIs were predicting the imminent fall of the capital, St. George's, but the pictures of General Hudson Austin's troops being led away in chains only depressed him. A young reporter dressed in a brand-new bush shirt and spotless white trousers crowed about how "America had kicked the Viet Nam syndrome at last," and the shopkeeper smiled sourly. War was a complicated business, perpetually testing human "loyalty, trust, and constancy." Toan repeated the words from the love letter in his pocket as though he had a lump in his throat, and when the reporter announced that President Reagan would give a major speech to the nation at 9:00 p.m., he merely grimaced. His little American flag lay untouched next to the cash register.

"Did you finish it?"

Toan pointed the remote at the TV and turned the set off. The American glanced up at the blank screen.

"Why'd you turn it off?" he asked, his mouth curved down in disappointment. "Aren't you glad we're whipping them?" He came close and eyed the Vietnamese skeptically. Phan Van Toan held his breath at his smell. "You *are* a loyal American now, aren't you?"

Toan flinched at the word "loyal," and his only reply was to turn the TV back on. The network had already returned to a soap opera. A man in a bar cupped a glass of whiskey in his hands and complained to the bartender about his wife, who was cheating on him. "You just can't trust *anyone*," the man whined, taking a deep drink. The bartender nodded and wiped the counter in front of him.

Phan Van Toan quickly clicked the TV off again.

"You did translate the letter, didn't you?"

Toan's eyes met the American's again, but he found it difficult to speak.

"Yes, I—"

He halted, and the American nodded as though he'd read his mind. He reached in his pocket and pulled out a crisp twenty-dollar bill folded over several times. He carefully unfolded it and smoothed it out on the counter. The odor of new money contrasted strangely with the man's smell. "I told you I could pay." He shoved the bill across to Toan.

The Vietnamese stared at it and colored with shame. But he reached under the counter and grabbed the translated love letter. *Dear Friend,* it now read, *it grieve me to write this, but you so far away and the night so cold. I afraid we can no go on like this. . . .* He passed the letter across to the American. The GI picked the translation up and scrutinized it, and Phan Van Toan shifted restlessly on his feet while he stumbled through it. When the man finished, he glanced down at the counter, where the twenty-dollar bill rested against the American flag. He gazed doubtingly at the shopkeeper.

"Aren't you going to take it?"

The front door swung open, and a chunky Glendale policeman stepped inside, followed by a blast of hot air and the smell of sizzling macadam. The cop was streaming with sweat. He nodded to the shopkeeper and proceeded at once to the soft drink cooler. His waistband radio crackled, and as he reached down to flick it off, Vi and his friend Jimmy entered the store. Phan Van Toan's mouth pinched up with worry. Vi must have gotten a lecture from his mother, for he avoided his uncle's eyes as he followed his companion to the back of the shop. The lump rose in the store clerk's throat again. Apparently they hadn't noticed the cop, either. Just then something pushed up against his fingers.

"Hey, if you don't want it, man . . ." The American's hand started to close over the money. Toan hastily snatched the bill out from under him.

"I take. . . . Thanks."

The American shrugged and drew an envelope from his pocket. He proceeded to slip the translation inside it. All of a sudden Phan Van Toan blanched and let the twenty-dollar bill fall to the counter. His knees wobbled, and his eyeballs bulged to the point of bursting. In the upper-right-hand corner of the envelope was a Mac Thi Buoi stamp. The shopkeeper blinked hard and zeroed in on it. Yes! It was the red 1000 piaster stamp, the missing jewel in his collection. Mac Thi Buoi had served against the French, uncovering traitors in her native village until she was arrested and put to death in 1951. Her loyalty and bravery had made her the pride of all Viet Nam, and now her stamps were worth as much as $600 each. Toan already had the brown 2000 dong stamp, the green 4000, even the blue 5000. But the red one, the color of precious blood, had slipped through his fingers once before, and now he couldn't believe it! His hand lurched forward and grabbed the American's wrist, at the same time his mouth began to water. The GI stared at him in surprise.

"What's wrong with you?"

"Where . . ." Phan Van Toan could barely talk. The word erupted from his mouth in a voice that was tinny and strained, and he shook as though he was suffering from a fit. "Where you get that?"

The American's brow wrinkled in confusion.

"What are you talking about?"

"Hey, what are you boys up to? Stop!"

The cry came from the other end of the store. Phan Van Toan raised his head. Several cans of mixed nuts and condensed soup on the shelves across from the magazine racks tumbled to the floor and began to roll around. Then the shelves themselves started to tremble, and the shopkeeper thought they'd been hit by an earthquake.

"Come back here!" the cop bellowed.

Vi and Jimmy ran out of the convenience store, and the policeman muttered a curse and tore off after them. Toan sprang from behind the counter and dashed out the door. The close stifling air and the stench of hot tar hit him hard, and he staggered and had to catch himself against a lamppost. He felt as disoriented as on that last panicky morning in Saigon.

Mai had come to him with tears in her eyes and pleaded with him to save Khach. Toan's brother, a policeman himself, was wandering the streets of the falling city, his loaded revolver in his hand, his face gaunt with grief and despair at the impending collapse of the South Vietnamese government. Toan rebuked her for her melodrama, but he'd already packed his things and was now waiting impatiently for the BFA branch to open on the ground floor of the Eden Arcade. Caught downtown by the curfew the day before and concerned about the deteriorating security, he'd stored the red Mac Thi Buoi stamp he'd picked up at the philatelist's market in Da Kao that afternoon in the bank's vault, then spent the night cleaning out his office. He reassured Mai and whisked her off to the American Embassy along with Vi. Then he hurried to the Eden Building and banged on the shuttered bank gate for twenty-five minutes, until another Saigon policeman, one of the last to leave his post besides Khach, came along and ordered him away. By then he scarcely had time to make it to the Embassy himself. He arrived just as Mai's helicopter, the next to the last, took off from the roof and arced toward the ships waiting in the South China Sea. The Marines who pulled him on board the final chopper attributed his anguish to the sad ending of the war. . . .

"Wait! Wait!" he shouted, to no one in particular, as he raced up Broadway. He sped past the Salvation Army Thrift Shop and a furniture store fronted with date palms and orange trees, and then the squat alabaster pile of the Glendale Galleria loomed in the distance. He saw the two boys skittering ahead on their skateboards, the fat cop puffing along behind them and shouting for them to stop. Toan hobbled after them as fast as his legs would carry him. He soon overtook the policeman, who'd stopped to mop his brow and was yelling into his radio for backup.

"No, no!" Toan said, impulsively grabbing him by the sleeve. The policeman wheeled angrily.

"You want trouble, too? Those kids just stole a *Playboy.*" The radio spluttered, and the policeman barked into it. Phan Van Toan's heart pounded with trepidation.

"Please, Officer, no catch. Please!"

He whipped his arms about as though he was trying to fly, and the policeman lifted his mouth from the radio and stared at him. The cop's face was streaked with sweat. His eyes narrowed at Toan the way the American GI's had.

"You know those boys?" he demanded.

Toan squinted past the policeman's broad shoulder. Vi and his friend were fading fast. In the boiling heat which swirled up from the pavement they looked as though they were floating off the ground and spinning away, just as those last two helicopters must have looked to the people left behind on the ground as they flew swiftly toward the coast. To the living ones, that is. Phan Van Toan let out an agonized groan.

"Do you?" the policeman repeated.

The store clerk felt as though a hot iron was pressed against his heart. Later that day, when he and Mai were reunited on the flight deck of the *Hancock,* he told her of his failed mission and then had to listen while his sister-in-law wept inconsolably and clasped Vi to her chest. The six-year-old boy stared at his uncle with frightened eyes. Fortunately, Mai was still prostrate with misery the next morning when the newspapers arrived, with pictures of the fall of Saigon splattered all over their pages. Phan Van Toan took one look at the photo of the Saigon police-man who'd shot himself in front of the war memorial statue across from the National Assembly and immediately flung the journal he was reading into the sea. His face was whiter than the whitecaps which plashed against the carrier's side. . . .

The cop thumped him on the chest.

"Did you hear me?"

Toan suddenly remembered the Mac Thi Buoi stamp. He broke out in a sweat of his own.

"No, Officer," he said, his voice frantic with misgiving. "I no know them."

———

The twenty-dollar bill was still lying beside the American flag, but Phan Van Toan's whole body tingled with apprehension as he scoured the counter, the floor, the cash register, and even the drawers underneath it, although he had to unlock each one. Then he scrambled desperately from aisle to aisle, on his hands and knees like a dog, flinging aside the cans of nuts and soup which Vi and his friend had knocked over during their escape from the store. He found it harder and harder to breathe as he went along, and he gasped in frustration when something white poking from beneath the soda cooler turned out to be only a discarded grocery list. He was so sweaty now his palms slid on the floor, and then he slipped and his head cracked against the tiles. He swore furiously, and his face pulsed with pain as he lifted it and tasted blood from a cut on his lip. The sight of it, red as his beloved Mac Thi Buoi stamp, brought him to the verge of tears. He was barely able to stumble back to his stool behind the counter, where he held his head in his hands and crumpled in defeat.

A voice boomed from the television, which the American must have turned on again while he waited for Toan to return. The shopkeeper glanced up. A reporter stood in front of a bullet-riddled statue of Maurice Bishop in the middle of St. George's. In breathless tones he announced that the general in charge of the invasion was about to describe the brilliant strategy by which the Americans were winning the war. The words had little effect on Phan Van Toan, whose head was still throbbing. But a body lay in plain view beside the statue, and a spasm shook the store clerk when he spotted it. The newsman chattered on about the one-sided battle for Grenada, and Toan wondered why he hadn't noticed the dead man sprawled almost at his feet. Flies buzzed about the corpse, which was beginning to bloat and blacken in the hot tropical sun, and Phan Van Toan shivered all over, as though the stench of decay had seeped right through the television. Don't just stand there! Why don't you *do* something? Take it away, for God's sake! He averted his eyes.

The shopkeeper felt as though a sledgehammer pounded on his brain. Blood raced painfully to his temples. He waited until the agony passed, then raised his eyes to the TV again. The statue was still there, as was the reporter, but not the body. It had simply disappeared, back to the darkest regions of Phan Van Toan's mind. With unsteady hands he reached for the remote and turned off the television.

three

THE SON RETURNS

Disobedient sons cost so much, Mother Binh thought. Her eyes darted from the sweat-dappled back of Mr. Lam, the rickshaw driver, to the black lacquer box in her lap. She lifted the lid and peeped at the dried-up umbilical cord resting on a piece of white gauze. Her nose pinched up at the smell of formaldehyde. Preceptor Vu would charge a pretty penny for bringing him her son's umbilical cord, but how else could she get Dat home when he'd refused to see her yesterday?

The crimson sun bloodied the paddy fields shimmering with transplanted rice shoots and dipped toward the pine trees of the Bo Drang forest. Mother Binh clutched the box tighter.

"Faster, faster!" she yelled. She leaned forward in her seat and peered anxiously at the shadows deepening behind the spurge hedge. "Before the ceremony is over. I must get my son back."

Mr. Lam pumped his legs harder. It was Wandering Souls Eve, and if Preceptor Vu did not bury the umbilical cord in

31

Mother Binh's yard by nightfall, she'd have to wait another year. The rickshaw rounded a bend in the Nam Hoa highway, and Mother Binh spotted the Temple of Holy Blessedness in the distance. She leaned back and sighed.

Her request was so simple: come take care of your mother. What could be more reasonable? Dat had been very dutiful before he went to Hue two years earlier, sweeping the hearth at Tet, dusting the family altar like a girl, preparing her betel nut every night when she returned from the market. Mother Binh liked to remind her friend Quoc of these little attentions. Quoc's own son Phi was a ne'er-do-well who pimped for a whorehouse in Hanoi and never even wrote. Mother Binh would choose a moment when Quoc was complaining about Phi's latest run-in with the police to talk about Dat's rectitude. The emperor had presented him with the "Model of the State" award, for example, or his essay on the moral beauty of politicians had won first prize in the courtiers' competition. Mother Binh's chest would surge as she read aloud his letters, while Quoc sat there grinding her teeth.

How they would envy her now! A first rank mandarin, the emperor's aorta, come home to look after his aging mother!

The rickshaw trundled into Tran Bong, and Mother Binh stuck her head up so her neighbors could see her arrive in state. She tried to look important as Mr. Lam huffed to a halt in the center of the village, but her fingers toyed nervously with Dat's last note. She quickly shoved it into her duffel bag, sprang from the rickshaw, and strode toward the temple.

"Mrs. Binh!" Mr. Lam shouted. "My money!"

Mother Binh winced. She turned and fished a one piaster note from her pocket. She shoved it into his hand.

"The fare from Nam Hoa is *two*," Lam said. He glared at her mistrustfully.

"Two nothing," Mother Binh replied. "I have no more." She spun aside to prevent him from spotting the wad of banknotes in her pocket.

"Cheapskate!"

Mother Binh shook him off and turned to the temple porch again. Her heart jumped. Preceptor Vu had finished his prayers and was walking away.

"Father Vu! Father Vu!" she called. "Wait!"

She leaped onto the porch. Preceptor Vu wheeled. A green and red dragon which snaked around the column next to him glowered at her. It was as though Master Vu had two sets of eyes.

"Oh, Father," Mother Binh burst out. "I'm *so* glad I caught you." She noticed his frown. "I hope . . . I'm not keeping you."

A muffled dinner gong sounded in the refectory behind him. The smell of stewed mung beans wafted across the porch.

"What *is* it, Mrs. Binh?" Preceptor Vu said, turning his head and breathing in the sweet aroma. His sharp tone made her feel glum. It was not what she expected from a man who should have appreciated her position. In his letters Dat had urged her to curry favor with Preceptor Vu, District Chief Ho, and other village notables. *Canaille* like Quoc and Lam were to be scrupulously avoided.

She thrust the lacquer box forward.

"Please, Dear Master," she said. Her voice quavered.

Preceptor Vu cautiously eyed the box. Then his face brightened.

"An offering for Buddha?"

Mother Binh shook her head.

"My remembrance of my son Dat, Dear Master," she said. "To call him home."

Master Vu joggled the box. His frown returned. "What's this rattling?"

Anxiety rose up in Mother Binh's throat. The crisis was upon her. What if he refused her now?

"As you know, Great Master," she said, hurriedly stepping forward, "Dat is the devoted confidant of the emperor." She scanned his face, but the mention of the royal name appeared to leave no impression. "His *Majesty,*" she emphasized, speaking loudly now and wheeling to face the crowd, "holds him in *very* high regard." Her countenance fell. The crowd had melted away. She turned back to the master.

Preceptor Vu opened the box. He crimped his nose and snapped his head back. A jackdaw looking down from a nearby kapok tree cawed in astonishment.

"This is most . . . irregular, Mrs. Binh," he said. "I cannot say prayers for the return of your son over . . . *this.*" He shoved the box back as though it housed an incubus. "It belongs in Nam Hoa, not here."

Mother Binh felt boxed in with dismay. "How much?"

Father Vu smacked his lips. "Twenty piasters."

Mother Binh flinched. She fondled the piasters in her pocket, two years' savings from selling corn cakes in the Tran Bong market. Was it worth it? She thought of Dat sweeping into the village on one of the emperor's palanquins, followed by a train of lackeys, concubines, and packhorses laden with gifts. Her hand peeped tentatively from her pocket, then slowly came forth. Preceptor Vu had to pry the fingers loose.

"And five more for Buddha," he said, snatching another bill before she could tear away her hand. Mother Binh gulped down her chagrin. A disobedient son was expensive indeed.

———

From her first moment in Hue the day before, Mother Binh seemed to swell with the city, expanding to fit the rickshaw that hustled her through the streets and taking in the new sights, sounds, and colors with gusto. A royal zither player whistled at her outside the old citadel, and Mother Binh blushed like a flame tree. Once she'd had her way with every man in Tran Bong, and even now the rice merchant Ngu, richest man in Thua Thien province, still sent her apricot branches at Tet with the message "To the loveliest blossom of all" pinned to the bark. She smirked mincingly at the musician and motioned the cabbie to drive on. At the Noontime Gate a scholar in scarlet robes and floppy hat gazed wistfully at her, as though he read in her eyes her sensitive intellect, her artistic soul set free and floating over the city like the sweet breezes of the Perfume River. She forgot about Tran Bong and its clunky ways. This was *her* town.

It was 10:00 a.m., too early to disturb the lifeblood of the state. Mother Binh squinted hard and tried to pick out Dat's apartment in the crenellated towers of the imperial city. They all looked alike. Surely the emperor kept Dat close by him, perhaps in the Palace of Supreme Peace itself. Mother Binh closed her eyes and was instantly inside. She knelt at the throne, swept aside the panels of her *ao dai*, and curtsied majestically. The empress and her daughters clapped their hands in delight, plunged to the ground, and bowed to Mother Binh in turn. The emperor stood with a flourish and handed her into the reception hall himself, where all eyes devoured her with envy. Mother Binh rose in the rickshaw like a balloon about to take off.

"Hey, old lady, you wanna stay here all day?"

Mother Binh's eyes opened. She flashed the cabbie a withering look.

"In *my* village, young man," she admonished, "we do not call our elderwomen 'old lady.' We adhere to the ancient forms of respect."

Mother Binh liked this turn of phrase. It sounded regal.

"Where to, then, honorable *Aunt-ie?*" the driver said. "Though it's *your* money." He shrugged.

At the mention of money Mother Binh shifted uneasily. She clawed at her purse to make sure it was still there.

"Well, drive me across that bridge there," she said, pointing. "And be quick about it."

The rickshaw driver laughed.

"The Golden Water Bridge? You must be joking, lady." He eyed her with pity. "Only a *nha que* from the villages would think such a thing. That's reserved for the emperor."

Mother Binh bridled. Imagine him mistaking her for a pot-walloper like Quoc! But how could she get in to see her son?

"Fancy *you* showing up," Dung said, when Mother Binh appeared on her doorstep fifteen minutes later. She abruptly turned her back on her sister-in-law and shuffled to the stove. Hot oil spat in the wok which looked to Mother Binh like an inverted metal conical hat. She wondered how anyone could cook in such a thing. Dung caught her staring at it.

"Well, all right, you can stay out there, by the cistern." She waved her spatula in the direction of a lean-to which Mother Binh spied through the back door. "Just don't snore. And *this* time, pay me." The visitor frowned, but Dung just shrugged, like the rickshaw driver Binh had sent back to the citadel with a note for Dat. Shrugging seemed to be a Hue habit. "I'm not running an almshouse, you know."

Mother Binh tried to carry her head high as she carted her duffel bag into the back, but she felt she was slinking like a thief. She hadn't wanted to come here, but Dung was the only person she knew in the capital besides Dat. And she had to wait *somewhere* for her son's reply.

Mother Binh had never been able to lord it over Dung. Dung felt her brother Kim had stooped too far in marrying her. A common village huckster, with blackened teeth and the smell of the barnyard! Kim liked to throw this in his wife's face whenever he drank, which was often. Rumor had it he'd been drummed out of Hue for dealing in contraband rice, though to hear him tell it the "siren's song of love" had called him to the boonies. The happy couple put down roots in Nam Hoa, where Mother Binh occasionally caught her husband digging in the yard late at night. In an unguarded moment she'd mentioned she had a "little something" stowed away for a rainy day. Kim was looking for a spot to bury their children's umbilical cords, he said. Just in case. Mother Binh had her doubts.

Then his sister got a job as the emperor's twelfth concubine's seamstress.

"*Now* who's the clodhopper, you witch?" Kim said to Binh. He stole some money from her and went on a binge that saved her further trouble. Dung couldn't make it to the funeral. It was too lowering.

Kim had died years ago, and Dung hadn't seen her sister-in-law very much in the meantime. But unwanted relatives had a way of showing up when least expected. . . .

"Letter for you," Dung said, about an hour after Mother Binh lay down for a snooze.

Something feathery plopped onto Mother Binh's chest. She quickly opened her eyes. Sweet perfume wafted from the note, jarring with the kitchen grease. Mother Binh's heart skipped as she sat up and picked at the imperial seal. She waved her hand in the air to dismiss her sister-in-law, then noticed that Dung had already returned to the kitchen.

Honored Mother:
Your respectful son Dat begs his honored mother to understand that His Imperial Highness the Emperor does not approve of "personal contacts" between his servants and individuals outside the royal palace. Such contacts, in the words of His Great Nobleness, "lack dignity." Your respectful son Dat therefore regrets that his official duties preclude him, etc., etc.

Mother Binh read no further. Tears blinded the elaborately scrolled letters. How could he *do* this to her? The bubble of her state reception burst in an instant. She plunked down on the bed like a punctured bag of rice and felt as though her life was spilling out in front of her. The bed squeaked under her weight. She barely had time to wipe her eyes before Dung appeared in the doorway.

"Anything wrong, dear sister?" she asked, hands on her hips. "Got the sniffles?"

Mother Binh rammed Dat's note into her duffel bag and sprang from the bed. She cleared her throat and stretched on her toes. She was not about to sag in front of Dung.

"Nothing's wrong," she said. "Absolutely nothing." She plucked the bag off the bed. "Dat can see me now, that's all. The emperor wished to prepare . . . a proper reception for me."

A disbelieving smirk formed at the edges of Dung's mouth. Mother Binh edged around her and tramped toward the door.

"With your duffel bag?" Dung taunted.

Mother Binh wheeled.

"Of course," she shot back. "*I've* been invited to stay in the Everlasting Longevity Palace." She tossed her head and blinked in satisfaction when Dung grimaced. This was a home thrust. Commoners were not allowed inside the Dien Tho.

She turned and marched through the door. Her step was much lighter now. Hadn't she just received a letter from the emperor's favorite?

———

The minute she stepped into her hut after Preceptor Vu buried Dat's umbilical cord, Mother Binh dug the photographs of the Imperial Palace and of Dat in his mandarin uniform out of her duffel bag. She wiped them off and stepped to the yellow balau cabinet in the middle of the room. She shunted aside the pictures of her parents on the top of the cabinet and positioned their replacements in the exact center, where they would attract most notice. Then she stood back and admired them the way a stage director might admire his scene set.

Happiness flooded Mother Binh's entire being. She'd suddenly remembered that Wandering Souls Day was coming up while she was on her way home from Hue the previous evening. She stopped overnight in Nam Hoa and dug up Dat's umbilical cord from the yard where Kim had buried it. The decision to do so had been truly inspired, well beyond the limited capacities of Quoc and the other Tran Bong hicks. Mother Binh rubbed her lips together in satisfaction. Now she'd be able to draw Dat home in spite of the emperor and his snooty ways.

Just then, a duck waddled in from the garden and stood by the duffel bag. It popped its head up and seemed to stare at

Dat's picture with his mother's rapture. Mother Binh flashed it a grateful look, but then the look changed to one of astonishment when the duck rummaged in the duffel bag and snatched Dat's note along with a rice cake. She sprang forward, but the duck quickly dropped the rice cake and skittered from the hut with the note in its beak. Mother Binh thought of chasing it, but then her eye caught on Tuyen's "Guide to the Royal Palaces of Hue" peeping from the bag. She glanced at the mantel clock. It was eight. She'd invited Quoc and some others at nine to learn about the emperor's hospitality. She grabbed the book and plumped down at the dining table. She had a lot of facts to master. When she caught the duck, she'd cook him for dinner.

"He's quite the success there," she said to Quoc an hour later, glancing at Dat's photograph. She'd frowned when Quoc showed up alone but figured the rest of the villagers were cowed by her new grandeur and would come along later. She made sure Quoc was looking at her and then cooed with maternal pride:

"Such a devoted councillor. His Highness and I almost fell out over who needed him more, his mother or the state." She burst into a little laugh. "No thanks, dearie," she said, shaking her head at Quoc's cheap *nep* wine. "I'll take *this*."

She picked up a bottle of Napoleon VSOP from the table next to her and poured out a tumblerful. Then she recorked it and set it down.

"His Great Nobleness gave me this just as I was leaving," she said, tapping the bottle. In reality Kim had stolen the brandy along with some other items from the French consul in Nam Hoa while on his last binge. His liver caught up with him before he could enjoy it. "He's *such* a kind man. Not at all stuffy. Unlike what they say, you know."

Mother Binh's gaze flew to the photo of the palace. She tried to remember where she was supposed to have stayed.

"Oh yes, I was quite the queen in that . . . Grandmother's Palace of theirs." She leaned forward confidingly. "It's reserved for *very* special guests. Madame Doumer, the Governor-General's wife, was perfectly *furious* when she found out about it. She's been refused it three times, you know." Mother Binh clucked in triumph. "She was quite snippy with me at the state dinner."

Madame Doumer would have been surprised to learn of Mother Binh's existence, let alone her "state dinner." But Quoc's eyes were as big as dinosaur eggs, and Mother Binh was satisfied.

She closed her eyes. "Goose down pillows, lotus bathwater, lackeys waving palm fans, pedicurists from Paris. . . ." She exhaled a dreamy breath and opened her eyes. Quoc was staring at the brandy bottle. Mother Binh edged it away from her.

"What's that?" Quoc asked.

The rudeness of the question grated on Mother Binh's nerves. The courtiers in Hue had been so refined. . . .

"They say *keski-say* at the palace, my dear," she said didactically. Quoc still stared at the Napoleon.

"I'm thinking of selling my baskets," Mother Binh quickly added, laying a protective hand on the neck of the bottle. "Business isn't the thing for me now. Do you know anyone interested in buying me out?"

"You're giving up the concession?" Quoc asked. She eagerly examined her friend's face. Mother Binh snickered. Quoc was as distractible as a puppy.

"Oh, yes. You see, Dat doesn't approve. In fact, in his last letter he urged me to be sensitive to our . . . altered circumstances. Brought about, of course"—and here she batted her eyelashes—"by his impending return." Mother Binh now rushed her words to keep from stammering. "We must be prepared to assume our rightful place in the community when that happens."

She rose up in her chair, and Quoc sank down accordingly, like a seesaw. Mother Binh was quite pleased with her magnificent new tone. Who would recognize the corn vendor in her now?

"Well, you will keep *me* in mind, won't you?" Quoc said. "After all, we've been friends for such—"

A low tapping sounded on the door, so soft, so tentative, that for a moment Mother Binh had the absurd idea the duck had come back to return Dat's note. The knock sounded again. Mother Binh gazed at Quoc, then called in an exaggerated contralto: "Come iiinnnnnnnnnnnnnnnnnnnnn!"

The door swung to with a creak. Standing in the dim light, dressed in a filthy peasant's smock and cheap pantaloons, with a shabby hat pulled low over his brow and a battered valise in one hand, was her son Dat.

Mother Binh's jaw dropped. She blinked several times. Was it really Dat? Her heart beat rapidly, but then she shrank back in her chair. Ghosts were known to pop in on their families like this, unannounced, and hadn't his note convinced her she was not likely to see him in the flesh again? She trembled all over. He certainly wasn't dressed like the emperor's favorite. Spirits sometimes did peculiar things to throw their loved ones off guard, in case they were tempted to forget them. Mother Binh swallowed hard and found it difficult to look at him. But then she recovered. The smell of alcohol rapidly filling the little room was very real indeed. So were Dat's hiccups. She glanced quickly at Mrs. Quoc, who stared stupidly at the new arrival. *She* had to be kept in the dark in any event. Mother Binh leaped from her chair and pranced toward Dat the way the empress herself might.

"My soooonn!" she said, in her phony contralto. "I *knew* you would return." She tried to sound sincere, and felt from the idiotic expression on Quoc's face that she succeeded.

"How good of you to take time from your official duties to pay your respects to your old mother. And her *friends,* too."

She condescended a nod at Quoc to tip her off to her good fortune, then turned back to Dat, who slouched in the doorway. What was he up to?

Quoc coughed nervously, and Mother Binh looked at her. Her friend squiggled about in her seat as though debating whether to rise or kneel. Mother Binh extended her hand.

"Come, dear Quoc," she said, with a little laugh. "You needn't be so timid. Greet the boy. The life and soul of the empire may depend on him when he's *down there,* but here in Tran Bong he is just a villager, like his mother."

She yanked her friend to her feet. Quoc scraped toward Dat like a whipped dog.

"Hello, great king, er, great sir," she sputtered. "I hope you had a pleasant—"

"That's enough," Mother Binh interrupted, laying a heavy hand on Quoc's shoulder. She noticed with alarm that Dat wouldn't look at them. His strange outfit still bothered her. And the alcohol on his breath wasn't Napoleon, either. She turned to her neighbor. "You may go now."

Mrs. Quoc glared at her hostess, muttered something, and skulked toward the door.

"Such a pretentious old hag," Mother Binh said, glancing at Dat. The door banged. Mother Binh started. "These people must learn their place," she sniffed. She eyed her son uncertainly. Why didn't he say something? What was he doing here? Her brow suddenly cleared. The umbilical cord had worked! Its magnetic power must be enormous indeed, since Preceptor Vu had buried it only a few hours before.

"Oh, my son!" she exclaimed, coming up to him. "Welcome home at last!"

Dat sprang back from her. He still clutched his valise.

"'Snot home, Mother," he said. "Leastways, won't be for long." His gaze flew to the door. "I'm on the run."

"*Non*sense, my son," Mother Binh said. Yet her voice wavered. "Of course this is home. You have come back to me, as Father Vu said you would." She clasped her hands. "Oh, what a good, wise man!" Dat did not reply. "Come, we must inform him of your return. He is the only person worthy to receive you."

Dat's valise thunked to the floor. He plopped down on the trundle bed by the door and hunched his shoulders against his mother's advances like a bristling porcupine.

"You're not paying attention," he complained. "I'm on the run, I said. . . ." His throat stuck. "I've been selling the emperor's goods on the black market."

Mother Binh flicked her ear, hoping she hadn't heard right. It was perilous to listen to such ravings. The poor boy must have overworked himself down in Hue, straining his sensitive nerves. She had to soothe him into reason, not let him sink into irrational fantasy.

"What an imagination!" she scoffed. "Come, no more foolish chatter. You have had a long journey, my child. Tomorrow we will celebrate your return." She snapped her teeth ferociously as she recalled how Quoc had practically slammed the door in her face. The impudent creature! "We shall invite only the cream of the village. Then we shall set you up properly."

———

Mother Binh had difficulty sleeping. Strange ideas buzzed around in her head like flies on a grimy water buffalo. The thought that Dat might be a common thief unsettled her. There had to be a mistake! Hadn't he written her on the emperor's own stationery just the day before? Had he stolen *that,* too?

Tomorrow's reception would be delicate. Dat was on holiday, in need of rest, and was not to be tired out with frivolous questions. That was it! She'd gussy him up in the nice French suit Kim had pinched from the Nam Hoa consul, and the neighbors would be stricken dumb. And if he had to take off suddenly, well, the emperor found he couldn't get along without him. Mother Binh only hoped the cops wouldn't come looking for him. That could be difficult to explain.

Dat snored drunkenly on the trundle cot. Mother Binh kept a watchful eye on him. He'd insisted on sleeping by the door, saying he'd have to go pee in the night, but she suspected he might use the opportunity to sneak off. She'd caught him toping from a small flask right before he lay down, but didn't say anything. He'd have to sober up for the party, though. . . . She drifted off at last.

A noise jarred her awake, and Mother Binh's dream floated away. The emperor's eldest daughter, Lao, had been bathing her feet in lotus water. Nong, the royal dwarf, had been stuffing her with bonbons. Mother Binh rubbed her eyes and glanced at the trundle cot. Dat sat bolt upright, his body rigid as a pointer's.

"What *is* it, my son?"

"Shh!"

Mother Binh listened. Voices rumbled outside, and lights flickered under the door frame. Her brow furrowed, then cleared. The emperor himself had come to install Dat in his new duties! She sprang up in bed, licked her hair down with her palm, and straightened out the creases in her nightshirt. But why had he picked such a strange hour?

"Come, my son," she whispered, flitting to the trundle bed. "It is your time."

"Shh!" Dat said again. A loud rap on the door. Dat sprang to his feet and slunk behind his mother, very unlike an emperor's pet. Mother Binh looked questioningly at him but puffed her chest out nonetheless.

"Come in," she said, turning to the door. She backed toward the dining table, where His Highness would see her in the warm light of the spirit lamp, and felt Dat patter along behind her. She drew herself up by the table, coughed slightly, and called with more authority, "Why don't you come in, Your Majesty?"

The door swung open.

"Your Majesty nothing, you old fraud." Mrs. Quoc cried. "We've had enough of your blustering." Someone behind her yelled, "Yeah! That's right!" Mother Binh's heart snagged on the upbeat. Quoc stepped forward and brandished her lantern like a weapon. "You and your worthless son! Clear out!"

She shook a dirty paper. Mother Binh gasped. It was Dat's note.

"Yeah, clear out, you phony!" Mr. Lam yelled. "The emperor's guest indeed!" Tears sprang to Mrs. Binh's eyes. The ingrate! Hadn't she paid him liberally for carting her about?

"Move along!" other voices said, behind the leaders.

"But my dear friends!" Mother Binh said. She cupped her hands imploringly.

"We're not your *friends,*" jeered an old woman who'd once accused Mother Binh of stiffing her on her rice bill. She shook her fist. "The idea!"

The spirit lamp leaped in the breeze which rose behind Mother Binh, and her shoulders sagged as she picked out the endless crowd collected outside her door. She cried out in dismay and turned. Instinctively she stretched her arms out.

"My son! Protect me!"

Her hands clutched empty air. Dat had slipped through the back door.

———

Mother Binh hunched down in the shed behind her hut and listened. They'd tossed her out, along with Dat's valise, and said they expected her gone by daybreak. She heard them combing through her home, looking for whatever they could find, and she leered as she picked up their muttered curses. Dat had pilfered the Napoleon from under her nose and stuffed it in his valise in preparation for his departure. He must have pocketed her savings, too, for she couldn't find a single piaster. What a rogue! She didn't know whether to be angry or proud. Mother Binh uncorked the brandy bottle and took a long satisfying swig. He was still her son, after all. The duck was the real villain.

Mother Binh leaned out of the shed and peered at the hut. Lights flickered inside. *Nitwits! See what good it does you!* She peeped at a little mound of earth beside the banyan at the back of the yard. Later, when they were asleep, she'd creep from the shed and dig up the lacquerware box containing Dat's umbilical cord. "Fools," she said aloud. "You forgot that, didn't you?" She'd have no trouble duping some poor slob into buying the cord. Mothers wanted their children back all the time. Mrs. Binh thought about her absent son with deep affection. He'd be proud of her. A skillful salesperson could sell anything on the black market.

four

THE BLACK PHANTOM

Thuy Van sensed Father Xuan's eyes on her as she stood above her mother's grave, and she could almost guess his thoughts. *A child that age should cry at these things.* She hiked her little sister Phuong, who *was* blubbering, up on her hip, and watched the priest closely as he swung the censer over the grave. Holy water showered the little rectangular mound like scented rain. This small gesture of respect took the place of Thuy Van's tears. She was as dry as a paddy field before the rainy season.

Opium, the black phantom, had killed her mother the night before, and nothing in Father Xuan's religion had been able to prevent it. Obedient to her mother's commands, Thuy Van used to prepare her pipes after school, lighting the crystal lamp with the inverted bowl, rolling the opium into a little ball, heating it at the end of a needle, and watching it bubble brightly in the reversed bowl as her mother slowly inhaled. From time to time Thuy Van unburdened her conscience-stricken soul to Father Xuan, who assured her that God would intervene and save her mother at last. Now the girl felt robbed as well as guilty. She wheeled from the grave and the priest, tearing the mourning band from her forehead as she did so. She let it fall to the ground.

"Thuy Van!" Father Xuan called. "A word, if you please!"

The girl's spirits flagged as she unwillingly turned back. Father Xuan was the sole pastor for the thousands of refugees crowded into Saigon's largest shanty town, and she'd grown up believing in him and the power of his God. But as Thuy Van gazed upon his compassionate face, her blood froze like a winter stream, as though with her child's instinct, clear, cold, and rational as ice, she understood at last the futility of his commiseration.

"What will you do now?" the priest asked anxiously, when the two children came up to him. Thuy Van made no reply.

"*Em oi?*"

Phuong still wept on her hip, but Thuy Van made no effort to wipe her tears. Father Xuan took a slip of cambric from his pocket, but then halted at the look on Thuy Van's face.

"We can take care of ourselves," the girl said shortly. Father Xuan seemed visibly dismayed at the hostility in her voice.

"But where will you go? How will you live?"

Thuy Van smiled ironically.

"Haven't you taught us that God will provide? Just as he provided for *her*?"

She could not look at him, nor could she look back at the grave. The muscles in her neck willed her head in another direction. But she heard Father Xuan shuffle on his feet.

"*That* did not come from God, my child," he said quietly.

She glanced at him finally, and sensed his thoughts again. *What has happened to my influence over her?* The priest had occasionally asked her to take the place of the acolytes who went missing at her age, fifteen, some to join the Viet Cong, others to escape the draft, and Thuy Van had always compliantly accepted. At one time she'd even considered becoming a nun. But that too was now buried.

"Such things—"

"Yes, I know," she interrupted, "such things come from *man*." The edges of her mouth wrinkled up in scorn. "But your God did nothing to stop it. So I intend—"

Suddenly she heard yelling and looked away from him. Just beyond the cemetery, separated from it by a snatch of chicken wire, was the garbage dump for Tan Son Nhut airport. Conical-hatted peasants scrabbled about among the mounds of rubbish several yards from where her mother lay. Broken TV sets, blenders, table fans, Pyrex dishes, bamboo furniture, vacuum cleaners, ceramic elephants with their trunks or floppy ears missing. Trash of the Americans and their wealthy Vietnamese allies. Two old women bickered over a porcelain flowerpot on the crest of one of the junk piles. Thuy Van stared at it, fascinated. *How could such a brittle thing survive?* she wondered. It looked as lovely and delicate as a lotus blossom atop a dung heap, as it glinted in the sunlight while the two old women yanked it back and forth. Thuy Van lowered her gaze to the newly dug grave, and her heart felt as though a thousand elephants had trampled all over it. Most of the fragile things she knew did not last long, in the war.

She noticed a man standing on the other side of the grave, his elbows on the chicken wire, his hands cupped together. He was dressed in black, like Father Xuan, but he was not a priest. And he was peering straight at her. Something in the way he looked at Thuy Van unnerved her, but also caused her to remember her unfinished sentence. She glared at Father Xuan.

"I intend to do something about it."

She clamped her lips together in determination and challenged the priest with her eyes to stop her. He looked at her uneasily, as though he believed her capable of anything.

"My child," he said mournfully, "such thoughts are sacrilegious. You must cleanse yourself of them."

Thuy Van shook her head.

"I am not your child," she said, but she was shocked suddenly at her impertinence. She glanced at the man on the chicken wire again, and was almost certain he was responsible for it. He nodded at her. She turned back to Father Xuan.

"And it is not *I* who needs to be cleansed."

The two of them stared at each other in silence for almost a full minute. Then Thuy Van's eyes darted once more to the chicken wire, but the man was already gone. Above where he'd been standing a crash sounded as the flowerpot slipped out of the grasp of the two women and smashed against a rusty oil drum. Shards flew in all directions.

"Damn you!" yelled one of the women, bunching her fist and advancing on the other. "Damn you to Hell!"

Father Xuan quailed as though Thuy Van had just spoken the same exact words to him. She gazed at him, then stiffened and brought her sister up onto her hip again, higher this time. As she marched off, she sensed Father Xuan's eyes on her one last time, full of pity and concern. And her shoulders stiffened all the more.

———

Thuy Van hung out in a bystreet across from a cinema in Cho Lon until sunset, with Phuong on her lap. She watched the rich Chinese enter and then, several hours later, emerge from the theater with a Vietnamese, or occasionally even an American or European, girlfriend on their arm, from the afternoon showing of "Cleopatra." She observed them from a bench hidden in a little alcove set back from the sidewalk. The alley behind her stank of cooking oil, fish sauce, and garbage, and the last put her in mind of her mother's funeral that morning. For a moment it seemed as though the tears which had held themselves back in a little alcove of her mind might flow at last. But they didn't. Instead her woe fixed itself on what had happened the night before. After her mother died and Thuy Van drifted off to sleep beside the body, someone stole into their shack on the edge of the drainage canal and made off with all the money Thuy Van had hidden under the floorboards and most of her mother's possessions. Thuy Van awoke with a start and spotted a black figure creeping down the stairs with its arms full, but she was much too terrified to do anything but let it slip away. It was as though God had not punished her sufficiently by taking away her mother. . . .

"*Chi oi*, I'm hungry!"

Phuong squirmed in her lap, and Thuy Van glanced down at her. Tears formed in the younger child's eyes, and the lines around Thuy Van's mouth hardened. Yet her voice came out soft.

"I know, Phuong. I know."

She gazed at the cinema. A crowd of patrons loitered on the sidewalk and waited for the next show to begin. From where she was sitting, and even in the waning light, Thuy Van was able to pick out the flashy Orient watches, the rings on the men's fingers, the bracelets sparkling on the women's wrists, and the necklaces shining like rings of golden fire around their throats. Her mouth pursed up in envy. Whenever her mother took the house money to feed the black phantom, Thuy Van and Phuong had to go without. They lived off whatever they could pilfer at the Gia Dinh market. Shards of cuttlefish mostly, the discarded scales of a dace on which a scrap of meat still stuck, some dried-up cabbage and a bit of leftover rice. . . .

"*Chi oi!*"

The voice was imperative now, and Thuy Van put her down and looked at her sternly.

"Stay here," she commanded, and the harshness of her tone stemmed Phuong's tears. Thuy Van stood up, straightened out the wrinkles in her pyjamas, and glanced hastily in a hand mirror set outside a barber's shop next door. She ran her fingers through her hair and arranged it as neatly as she could. Then, after a moment's hesitation, she unhooked the top button of her shirt and pulled it down just far enough to expose the curve of her breasts. She blushed in shame as she looked in the mirror again, but it was no good begging from the Chinese, and what would happen to Phuong if she got arrested for stealing? Once again her own tears threatened to overwhelm her, but she took a deep breath and forced them down. She stepped forward. Behind her Phuong whimpered. Thuy Van spun on her.

"I said stay here!" she shouted, then felt a pang at the core of her heart. She moved penitently toward her sister, who started crying once more. Thuy Van kindled with renewed annoyance and backed away.

"And stop bawling!"

She turned to the theater and sized up the women on the men's arms. What she was about to do terrified her, but she stepped resolutely forward again nevertheless. The voice which suddenly called behind her, and which when she turned back she saw came from a man who had just taken her place on the bench and brought Phuong up onto his knees, sounded to her like the voice of salvation.

"Wait! There is another way. Come back!"

———

Thuy Van followed the man uncertainly, while Phuong readily took his hand and held it tight as they walked along. Past a rice factory beside the Cho Lon quay, its lights blazing as the work of husking, packing, and sorting went on notwithstanding the late hour. Past junks and sampans laden with fowl and fruit from the Mekong Delta, along a back alley reeking of urine and rotted fish from the Cho Quan market, into a cul-de-sac along both sides of which tin shacks, like those in her neighborhood but stuffed with Chinese, crowded them in as though to suffocate them. Thuy Van heard the click of an abacus, the clatter of mah jongg tiles, the raucous laughter of gamblers, the catcalls of squabbling women, the weeping of a drunk. . . . The man sped on, then stopped in front of a door at the very end of the row and inserted a key. Inside, by the light of a flickering kerosene lantern which hung from a hook in the rafters, Thuy Van saw six children, dressed in black just like the man, all of them about her own age or younger. They looked at her, unsmiling, but she did not feel unwelcome.

"This is Chi Tam," the man said, the eighth child, and for a moment Thuy Van thought he was singling out one of the other girls, perhaps the one whose face first dissolved into a smile of greeting and whom she therefore instantly liked. Then she noticed that the man was looking at *her*.

"A new name for a new beginning," he said, and he also smiled. "Please, come and sit down."

He guided Phuong to a small workbench and let go her hand. Thuy Van didn't follow. They were in a fisherman's shack, she realized. Nylon nets, some of them with holes in them, lay scattered about the floor, and the man picked his way carefully through them as he came back to her. Two of the younger children sat astride a big spar buoy from which the paint was peeling, as though they were riding a hobbyhorse. She smelled caulk, gum resin, paint remover, and the mixture of strange odors made her head feel light. *What were they all doing here? And why did she need a new name?* She was surprised, but felt no fear.

"*Em hai, ba, bon, nam, sau, bay,*" the man said, pointing out the other children one by one, just like in a family. *Child two, three, four, five, six, and seven,* skipping the unlucky number one, the envy of the evil spirits that snatched eldest children from their parents and took them to the black parts of the earth to live forever. Anh Sau, the sixth brother, reached down and pulled Phuong up onto the spar buoy behind him, and together the three babies laughed and bounced up and down as though the buoy tossed on the waves again. Thuy Van observed them closely. Phuong had not looked this happy in months. Thuy Van wheeled to the man, who stood in the middle of the room, gazing at her again.

"Get acquainted with them," he urged, and she allowed herself to be led the way Phuong had and suddenly felt the great need of a child to be wanted. The others were smiling now also, and Thuy Van made an effort and smiled back. Several of the older children looked familiar, though they appeared not to know her. Thuy Van sensed that any questions she might ask them would only divide them, and so she kept quiet. Like Phuong, she simply had to accept.

"And then," the man said, the smile still fixed to his face, "we will talk about your past, and your future."

––––––

Cao Minh had worked as a croupier at the Emerald Palace, he told her, on Tran Hung Dao Street just before it turns into Dong Khanh. Right under the Hynos toothpaste sign. This was in 1955, eight years earlier, when Thuy Van's mother was twenty-five and the country was just beginning to suffer under the brutal rule of the Catholics, in the form of its autocratic president Ngo Dinh Diem and his sadistic brother Nhu. Cao Minh would arrive early, check with the super, a survivor of Dien Bien Phu, collect money from the caissier, and seat herself at one of the green velours tables which sparkled beneath the chandeliers like the lawn of a great chateau along the Loire. . . . The customers would come, French still, mostly, some Americans and Chinese, some Vietnamese of the upper classes, top brass and civil servants. . . . Cao Minh hated the work, the cigar smoke, the drunken muzzles which after a few hours would crowd around her, like wolves circling, probing for a weak spot, seeking kisses or something else. . . . But she had a family to think of, aged parents in Long Xuyen, a crippled sister, her two daughters, of whom she was the only support. . . .

Thuy Van sat bolt upright, across from the man, listening carefully. Her fingers played with a fishing line from which the hook had been removed. A child's lantern from the Mid-Autumn Festival dangled at the other end, which she later learned the man used as a kite to delight them, on windy days, outside on the wharf overlooking the Ben Nghe Canal.

"Deux soixante-dix, s'il vous plait," a man said to her one night, his French effortful and artificial. The drug-drunk eyes

of a Vietnamese colonel already in the process of converting his sloppy French into pidgin American stared at Cao Minh, wanting and appreciating her. He held out dollars to her, triumphantly, like the head of John the Baptist on the platter, and she eyed them not greedily but fearfully, this treacherous money of the new foreigner, and passed across a row of black and white chips in return.

"Merci," the colonel said, and suddenly sprang forward to give her a kiss. She yanked her head back, but a skein of her hair entangled itself in the cross around his neck and made her blush until it broke free. Angrily the man turned his back, but the smell of him and his money, the reek of his cigar and the stench of his bad luck, lingered behind. Cao Minh's chest heaved, she did not know why. But later, after he lost his money and she denied him again, he got his revenge by unleashing the black phantom on her. That at least she was not able to resist. Nor, eventually, was she able to deny him anything else. . . .

———

The man fell silent. Thuy Van shuddered at the tale she'd never heard. She remembered a man passing in and out of her childhood like a phantom, that was all. Phuong was too young. Doubt and disbelief clawed at the girl's heart, trying to gain a hold like desperate fingernails on a cliff face, but she knew it must be true. *Why would this man lie to her?* She felt wretched when she thought of all her mother's suffering, and turned quickly to Phuong, starving after the child's innocence. Her sister still bounced up and down on the spar buoy, laughing as hard as ever. Her oblivious happiness suddenly filled Thuy Van with anger. She turned to the man sharply.

"How do you know all this?" she asked.

The man's smile faded.

"It is our *business* to know such things," he said.

Thuy Van moved to the work bench which her sister had vacated minutes earlier to join Anh Sau and the other child on the buoy. Years seemed to have passed since then, and Thuy Van felt as though she'd just leaped the chasm into adulthood and that her sister was stranded behind her on the other side, lost to her forever.

"*Chi oi!*" Phuong suddenly yelled, between laughs, as though to prove her wrong. "Come play with us!"

But Thuy Van's feet felt lifeless, her mouth as though stuffed with pitch. She could not answer, and after a moment or two Chi Bay, the seventh sister, sitting behind Phuong, tickled her, and Phuong giggled and was lost to Thuy Van again.

The man approached.

"You told that priest you wanted to do something about it, didn't you?"

Thuy Van looked up at him in surprise. She felt a vague fear, yet it was not fear of this man. But again she wondered how he knew.

———

He was not hard to find, for he was a general now and entitled to a limousine. The man in the fishing shack had supplied Thuy Van with the license number and a full description of his habits. She waited in an alleyway off Duong Cong Quynh, along with Anh Hai, the eldest of the family. She heard the Continental limousine idling down the street, just above her heartbeat, which was as rapid as any other virgin's. As a precaution against discovery she, too, was dressed in black.

"Try to calm yourself," Hai whispered in her ear. "Are you sure you are ready? We can come back another night, you know."

Thuy Van vigorously shook her head. She did not want to disappoint the man, who'd supervised her training with a close, steady eye and told her the night before that he was relying on her, in a tone which clearly implied that failure would be unacceptable. Phuong would take time, of course. But she was progressing nicely on her hobbyhorse, he'd added sardonically.

"No," Thuy Van said, clutching the hilt of the knife in her pocket. There was someone else she could not disappoint, who also would have expected this of her. "I am ready."

"Psst!" Hai murmured, shortly afterward. "You see up there? The light just came on. They must be finished."

Thuy Van raised her eyes to the slatted window on the second floor, and her heart beat faster. Her palm felt sweaty on the knife handle, and she was afraid it might slip out of her grasp when the time came. She released it, removed her hand from her pocket, and wiped it on her shirt. Anh Hai nudged her and pointed.

"Now the hall light's on! They're coming!"

They're? Thuy Van felt a sudden numbness inside her. "What if the girl's with him?" she asked, her voice filled with anxiety.

Anh Hai's mouth turned down grimly, but he was looking at the limousine.

"Well, in that case you'll have to kill them both," he said. "Can you manage it?"

Thuy Van stepped back, her head pounding as though it might explode.

"But she hasn't done anything," she protested, then stopped when Hai flashed her a cutting look.

"None of them is innocent, remember," he said sternly, echoing the words which the man in the fishing shack had repeated to her so often. "But you're in luck," he added, pointing again. "Go now! And be quick!"

Thuy Van wheeled, but she was trembling badly. A man, big for a Vietnamese, staggered under the streetlight outside the prostitute's door. He was clearly drunk. An easy mark, if only she could get her feet to respond. She remembered the moment of her mother's death, the rattle in her throat confusing at first, as though she was still sucking on her pipe, then her eyes rolling back in her head and the blood gushing from her mouth like water from a broken dam. Thuy Van sprang forward. Her hand no longer shook.

She was up to him in an instant, just as he emerged from the streetlight, and she inhaled the stenchful alcohol, opium, and sex which dripped off him and almost caused her to gag and give herself away. But she took a deep breath and in another second the knife was in, swiftly, skillfully, just as the man had taught her, so skillfully in fact that the drunken general was too surprised to cry out and simply collapsed on the pavement and lay there, looking up, as Thuy Van knelt and slashed his throat from ear to ear. The blood didn't bother her as it splattered across her front. It was the cleanest thing about him, coming out, and it barely showed on her dark clothes.

But in another moment an intense horror at what she'd done rushed through her, and the thought that there were two beings who approved it, one in Cho Quan and the other with the Emperor of Jade, did little to comfort her. She was so distressed in fact that it was not until they were back at the fishing shack that she recalled the car horn blaring behind her as the two of them sped away, and figured out that Hai had simply not bothered to lift the dead chauffeur's head off the steering wheel. . . .

———

"Why the driver?" she demanded, the minute she stepped inside. Her tone was so fierce the children on the hobbyhorse stopped bouncing and glanced at her apprehensively. Phuong was not among them. The man in black had reversed himself and decided it was time she learned to sell flowers outside the city cafés where the foreigners congregated. Flower girls had had enormous success in the days of the French, with grenades hidden in their baskets of coreopsis and heliconia, but they had to be under a certain age to avoid arousing suspicion.

The man glinted at her. He watched as Thuy Van, with shaking fingers, washed the general's blood off under the faucet.

"He might have told," he said, his voice calm. "And besides, none of them is innocent."

Thuy Van flared up at the repetition of the formula thrown at her like a bone to appease a dog. She resented the casual manner in which the man said it, and the way he turned abruptly away as though to dismiss her.

"If no one is innocent, that means *you* aren't, either," she shouted to his back.

He wheeled, and his lips parted in a cat's smile.

"Guilt or innocence is not decided by you or me," he said. "Others make that determination."

"Who?" she snapped, but the look in his eyes caused her to back down.

"According to that theory," he went on, after a moment, "*you* have things to answer for as well." His voice held a trace of menace in it, like bad air lingering in a mine shaft. Thuy Van quaked as she peered at him. *What did he mean?*

At that moment Phuong rushed through the door leading from the wharf. She had a basket on her arm, and her eyes glittered with excitement.

"Chi Van!" she exclaimed, tugging her sister by the arm. But Thuy Van's eyes were cemented straight ahead. Phuong had to shake her hard to get her attention. "Guess what! Tomorrow they're taking me to Ham Nghi to sell flowers!"

Thuy Van merely stared at her briefly, then turned back to the man.

Suddenly he reached into his pocket and brought out a small amboyna box. Thuy Van convulsed when she saw it. It was the box which contained the opium Thuy Van had prepared for her mother every night, dutifully abetting her slow suicide. The girl shuddered, first with anger, and then, when she saw the way the man was looking at her, in absolute fright. Phuong glanced at her, concerned.

"Are you cold, *chi oi?*" she piped up. She nestled against her sister's side. "Don't worry. With my very first money I shall buy you a sweater! Tomorrow perhaps!"

Thuy Van watched in alarm as the man turned his gaze on her sister. She drew Phuong to her, instinctively, protectively, the way a mother draws close a child. The man returned the box to his pocket.

"Run along and get some rest now," he said to Phuong, patting her lightly on the head. "You've got a big day tomorrow. And *remember,*" he added, his voice becoming serious, "I'm counting on you."

Phuong turned pale at the expression on his face, but then, when he broke into a smile, she quickly smiled back. Thuy Van wanted to shove him away, but the muscles in her arms, her shoulders, felt as weak as rubber. The man looked at *her* now.

"And *you've* got a big day tomorrow, too," he said, taking her firmly by the arm. He stared meaningly at her, the way he had the first time she saw him. "Let's go outside and talk about it, shall we?"

———

"Why are you dressed like that?" Father Xuan asked. Thuy Van felt her stomach plunge from a great height at her failure to put on something white, the color of mourning, before she left the shack that morning. She ducked her eyes as though the priest was God himself, reading the secrets of her troubled soul.

"But it's no matter," Father Xuan continued, as they strolled along together. "I'm just glad to see you. I was worried when you and your sister disappeared like that."

Thuy Van searched for a pretext. "We couldn't pay the rent," she said at last. "You see, someone stole our things, and I didn't know how we would survive. . . ."

She let her voice trail off as the pain pinched her deep inside. Father Xuan glanced down at her compassionately, and his look immediately unleashed all the hatred she needed to feel for him. Thuy Van shuddered violently, just as she had in the fishing shack.

"Quick, child!" the priest said, guiding her toward the church. "You'll catch your death out here." He unlocked the door.

Thuy Van's head spun with the incomprehensibility of it all as Father Xuan led her to a pew in the front row and gently sat her down. A statue of Jesus on the cross loomed up before her on the altar, directly above a basket of flowers. Father Xuan hurried away to turn off the ceiling fan, but Thuy Van stopped shaking long before he came back. Her eyes feasted on the flower basket rather than on the more commonly accepted symbol of absolution. Suddenly she saw a little child carrying it, eagerly, confidently, toward a sidewalk café crowded with enemies: drug dealers, prostitutes, drivers, and priests, all of them, including the child, blissfully ignorant of the crimes for which they needed atonement. Thuy Van heard footsteps behind her. She reached into her pocket.

five

LOVE BENEATH THE NAPALM

Mr. Tu leaned forward on his haunches, and with the aid of a trowel, gently dug out a weed which had insinuated itself between two of his pansies. It was late afternoon. A sharp breeze broke from the Helderberg Mountains seven miles away. Winter was coming, and he greatly missed his native village of Long Dien, which would now be entering the long hot dry season. Mr. Tu did not look forward to the death of his flower garden and the eight long months of wait before he could bring it to life again. He shivered in his thin, second-hand flannel jacket, a gift from Mrs. Hai-li, the Chinese owner of the Golden Dragon Restaurant on the corner of Peach Street and Route 138 in downtown Schenectady. She paid Mr. Tu thirty dollars a week to tend the two square boxes which stood beside the stone dragons in front of the restaurant.

"Hello, Uncle," a voice said to his back, in Vietnamese. Mr. Tu arched his neck in surprise. It had been months since anyone had spoken to him, aside from Mrs. Hai-li, and more than a year since he'd heard his own language. He turned.

The girl gave a sharp little cry and stepped back. She placed her hand over her mouth and stared at him, her eyes wide. Mr. Tu's jaw puckered painfully as he flashed her the resigned little smile he gave everyone. If he had not been peering down at a nice bauhinia flower on the An Loc battlefield when the bomb hit, his eyes would have fried like eggs and he would never have seen the look his face always inflicted on strangers. But then he noticed how much the young lady standing over him resembled Le. She had the same lush black hair; the same doe-like, almond-shaped eyes; the same playful smile of a kitten toying with a coil of hemp, now that she had recovered from her shock. Even the tilt of her shoulders was the same as she leaned forward again. Mr. Tu's heart throbbed joyfully.

"Why, hello, Little Sister," he said, struggling to keep his voice from quavering. Mr. Tu then spotted the man beside her. He was American, and had looked away, of course.

"I like your flowers," she said. "Wait, Phil," she added in English, tugging her companion's sleeve. The American was big, blond, and handsome, though in Mr. Tu's opinion not as handsome as he himself had once been. Mr. Tu sensed the man's irritation at being stopped from the way his fist tightened around the restaurant door handle.

"Come on," the American growled. "I'm hungry. You can squawk with this guy later."

The girl blushed at her companion's comment and stepped back from Mr. Tu again. The implication that their tongue resembled the talk of chickens would have caused Mr. Tu to blush as well if the plastic surgeon who'd repaired his face after An Loc had left him any color to work with. This man reminded him unpleasantly of his induction training in 1971. The American advisers at the Thu Duc Military School had mocked his beautiful language, made fun of his eyes, his skin the color of Cham drums, his inconsequential stature. Their innuendos about the inadequate size of the Vietnamese male member filled him with humiliation and rage. Mr. Tu glanced at the beautiful girl again. Had she taken this blond ape because of the bulk of his penis?

"Hoa?" the ape said, nudging her arm. His voice whined with impatience, and Mr. Tu felt perversely tempted to goad him.

"So your name is Hoa," he said conversationally, leaning back on his haunches. He tapped his garden box with his trowel. "It's a name I like." He was tired of hearing only the Chinese word for flower.

The girl laughed like a wind chime tinkling nervously in a breeze, and the sound filled Mr. Tu with delight. Mrs. Hai-li carped at him constantly and gave him nothing but scowls.

"I can see that," Hoa said. Mr. Tu was impressed at how quickly she picked up on his implication. This girl was smart as well as pretty, just like Le. Mr. Tu sighed at the memory of his fiancée. He'd met her in 1970, shortly after his father died and he moved to Saigon. Le was studying at the Faculté des Lettres and living with an old aunt in Gia Dinh. Back then Mr. Tu was something to look at, and their courtship blossomed like his pansy patch in summer, until the day he was called up for duty.

Hoa crouched down beside him.

"Did you garden back . . . there?" she asked.

The word *there* coursed through Mr. Tu's veins like a spring flood rushing along the Mekong. He watched as she indolently ran her fingers through the dirt of one of the flower boxes and then carefully straightened out a pansy which had bent in the breeze from the Helderbergs. *A girl from the earth,* he thought with satisfaction, *a true Vietnamese.* Yet what was she doing with this American?

"Not after I went to Saigon," he replied. "The ground wasn't suitable, you see. And—"

He stopped talking. The girl had suddenly turned her head back over her shoulder. The American was staring at the street. Mr. Tu was disconcerted at the interruption but looked on.

A green Thunderbird convertible with the top down chugged along the street toward them and screeched to a halt just beyond the Golden Dragon. Russet-colored maple leaves churned up by the little car twirled to the ground beside a clapboard house across the street. Two teenage girls in the front seat, a blonde and a redhead, wheeled their heads and whistled at the handsome American. Hoa leaned toward Phil but then froze. The scowl which overspread his face when she began to talk to Mr. Tu had melted in a big smile. The redhead, who was slightly overweight and had a half-empty bottle of liquor in one hand, thrust her breasts forward in a gesture which Mr. Tu found both vulgar and inviting.

"Hey guys, wanna party?" she crooned, swaying in her seat.

She winked at Phil, who burst into a laugh.

"Later, girlie," he called, giving her a friendly wave. "Save it for dessert."

The redhead tittered, and the convertible took off. Mr. Tu's face saddened as the woman beside him knit her brow and glanced down at her own tiny breasts. Suddenly she jabbed Mr. Tu's trowel into the potting soil and almost tore off one of the pansies. She threw the trowel down and looked away. Mr. Tu hastily leaned forward to fix the flower, but it flopped forlornly on its side, its neck broken. His heart yearned for the girl. He shared her humiliation as though it was another mark of their national disgrace, like the size of his penis.

The American peered at the Thunderbird until it disappeared up the street. The wind whipped through the man's hair like an autumn breeze through wheat. Mr. Tu shook his head. Phil was just the kind of loon who would appeal to a superficial woman like the tramp in the convertible. Such swine never lifted their snouts out of the muck. Mr. Tu eyed Hoa longingly. How could the tow-headed lout *ever* understand this lovely girl who'd seen through his face to the very heart of him? Only a Vietnamese could appreciate such an exquisite gem. But still he was uneasy.

Phil glanced down, and his face stiffened in a frown.

"Come on," he said coldly, tapping Hoa's shoulder. "That's enough. Let's eat."

Hoa barely looked at Mr. Tu now.

"Goodbye," she said, but her voice was distant. Mr. Tu gazed regretfully at her as she rose to her feet. He was hoping for another smile, just like Le's, and felt a pang of disappointment when instead she turned and edged close to Phil. Yet he knew she had to keep up appearances, and he took comfort from the fact that she held her body rigid beside the American. Mr. Tu thought of the many conquests of his youth, when women had dropped into his lap like persimmons from an overladen tree. Of course she was standoffish, reluctant to look at him! No woman likes to struggle with her affections. But she was beginning to fall for him, Mr. Tu felt certain. He could tell that from the way she'd laughed at his little joke about her name. He had a sense of these things. They were both Vietnamese, after all, linked by bonds invisible to the Americans. Mr. Tu felt suddenly exhilarated. His soul had peeked through his blistered skin at her like a crocus through the snow. As he leaned back on his haunches again and watched them enter the restaurant, he realized he was in love.

———

"Let's row out to the middle of the pond," Le said, grabbing his arm.

It was March 1972. Mr. Tu, twenty-three and crisp in his new lieutenant's uniform, removed his spotless suede gloves, folded them neatly in half, and slipped them into his pocket. He turned to her and smiled possessively, like all acknowledged lovers, and led her carefully along the dock which jutted into the crescent-shaped water lily pond on the grounds of the Botanical Gardens. It was the trysting place of lovers, but the disastrous Lam Son offensive of the year before had thinned the ranks of males, and solitary females could not take pleasure in a spot like this. For the moment they had it all to themselves, although Tu had to report to his unit the next morning. A new North Vietnamese offensive was rumored.

When they reached the end of the dock, he unmoored a rowboat, got in, and assisted her to board. He seated her in the stern, sat down amidships, fixed the oars in the rowlocks, and shoved off.

"How I shall miss you!" Le cried, leaning toward him. Tears glittered in her eyes like sun-spotted diamonds glancing off the surface of the lily pond. Their marriage had finally been set for the following month. Le had waited patiently for two years with the old aunt in Gia Dinh while Mr. Tu finished his training. Now they would have to wait some more.

A doleful-sounding vespers bell clanged in a nearby Buddhist monastery, and Mr. Tu felt a weight upon his heart as heavy as the iron from which it was cast. The bell seemed to toll their final moments together. The sweet scent of jasmine and rare orchids from the greenhouse on the far side of the island toward which they were heading only added to his sadness, and he pulled at the oars with long desolate strokes, like a mourner lugging a funeral barge.

"Don't think about it, my dearest," he said bravely, but Le burst into a torrent of tears. Mr. Tu quickly rowed beneath the Japanese bridge which crossed over to the island and stopped beneath one of its arches. Here she could indulge her sorrow in peace. He made the boat fast against the bank and seated himself beside her. He kissed her eyes, her lips, drank in the warmth of her body, the panting of her breath. She was beautiful, and he was happy and sad at the same time.

"My big strong soldier," she wailed. "How I shall worry about you!"

Mr. Tu nodded grimly and drew her close. In their two years together in Saigon other women had tempted him to kick over the traces, as was only natural with a man of his looks, but Le had managed to hold the reins tight and keep him on course. Never had they imagined she might lose him to the war.

"You will take care, won't you, darling?" she said, her voice choking.

"Of course," he responded, trying to sound cheerful. He hoped she would not notice his trembling, however. He thought of his father, who'd been caught in an airstrike while out tending his rice field on a foot-powered paddy pump. All they found of him afterward was a white powdery residue which looked like the chalk dust on the erasers at the Long Dien village school. Mr. Tu gripped the gunwales hard to stop his shaking. His unit was headed into the Iron Triangle, the jaws of the tiger. Le would have plenty to worry about, and so would he.

"Oh, my handsome one!" she exclaimed, collapsing on his shoulder and breaking down completely. Mr. Tu slumped in his seat. His carefree days were over. She fluttered against his chest like the last bird before winter. . . .

The wind whistled off the Helderbergs again, and Mr. Tu shuddered and sloughed off the sad memory. He heard a noise and looked up. Mrs. Hai-li stood over him, staring down.

"What are you still doing here, blockhead?" she asked, her voice shrill. "Take yourself off."

She scanned the sidewalk for customers. Business had fallen off lately, and she blamed it on Mr. Tu's face. People lost their appetite when they saw him. The sidewalk was empty.

She turned back and frowned at him.

"Shove off now, that's enough for tonight," she said, waving him off the stoop with the back of her hand. "You'll frighten the whole neighborhood if you stay here after dark."

Mr. Tu rose reluctantly to his feet. He eyed the restaurant door and thought of the girl Hoa seated somewhere behind it. Would he ever see her again?

"And don't forget that trowel," Mrs. Hai-li scolded, pointing to the tool which was barely visible in the dim light. "If it rusts in the damp air, the replacement will come out of your pay."

Mr. Tu attempted to bite his lip. He leaned over and picked up the trowel, gazing fondly at his beloved pansies one last time as he did so. Their ugly little mugs reminded him of his own, and they comforted him in his distress as Mrs. Hai-li continued to berate him even while he trudged sadly away. Why had fate linked him to such a doltish shrew? Once he wouldn't have given her a second thought, but now he had to march to her tune, all because of An Loc. Truly his lot was a hard one.

When he stumbled into his darkened garret a few minutes later and switched on the light, the drabness of his lodgings further dampened his spirits. Rodents pattered behind the plaster, and the wind howled through a window gap covered with cheap masking tape. Boys who lived in the neighborhood had thrown a rock through the window soon after he moved in and then laughed at Mr. Tu's pink hairless skull when it peeped through the jagged hole. Mr. Tu shook his fist at them, but they just laughed harder and strolled away in a leisurely fashion to show they were not afraid of him. Afterward Mr. Tu kept his head covered with a New York Yankees baseball cap, but he still felt aggrieved. The boys were Vietnamese.

The wind moaned through the window crack again, causing Mr. Tu to shiver and fluttering the candle which stood inside a tiny spirit lamp on top of his bureau. He thought how nice it would be to have the girl from the restaurant to warm his bed, and then he stared at the photograph beside the spirit lamp. Le smiled alluringly at him from a painted Chinese background, a sprig of *mai* blossoms in her hand. He'd taken the photo himself, and at the time he was very proud of it. But after he parted from her that last day in Saigon, with the North Vietnamese inexorably closing in, Mr. Tu succumbed to the superstition that cameras took away a person's soul. . . .

———

"This is my favorite part," he whispered, leaning over in the crowded movie theater and touching Le's sleeve. It was April 30, 1975. On the wide screen in front of them a tall Chinese warlord, girded for battle, strutted about his palace bedroom, gesticulating wildly at his wife, who stood glowering in the middle of the room, her fists tightened in a bunch. In the far corner the warlord's favorite concubine lay weeping.

"Yes, *thuong toi,*" Le said, nodding. She kept her eyes on the screen. "Just let me watch, will you?"

Mr. Tu thrilled with pleasure when she called him "my beloved," words he had not heard since that sad afternoon in the Botanical Gardens three years earlier. Given the way she'd greeted him that morning, he would not have expected it.

She'd shrunk behind the statue of the Virgin Mary in the deserted square outside the National Cathedral to protect herself from the unknown mutant who kept calling out her name and insisting he was her fiancé. Mr. Tu was hurt and chagrined until she remembered his voice. But Le too had changed. She was dressed in a pricy Western miniskirt, her hair curled in false ringlets, her mouth and cheeks painted red as a *Hat Boi* actress's. Still, he had recognized *her* immediately.

A rocket screeched by overhead, close to the theater, and Mr. Tu instinctively ducked. When it hit, his and Le's seats, as well as those of the other patrons who'd come there hoping to escape the war, shook in their sockets, and several people cried out in dread. Le glanced at him anxiously, and Mr. Tu put his arm around her shoulder to comfort her. They clung to each other and watched the conclusion of "Endless Passion," quaking whenever another rocket hit. . . .

———

Mr. Tu spotted Hoa from the far side of Liberty Street, late in the afternoon, near closing time. She was sitting in a chair by one of the tall library windows, reading something and basking in the rays of the declining sun. The gardener darted between some fast-moving cars and gained the other side of the street. He peeped in at her from several feet away, his heart pounding. With her head bowed over a magazine, her face at an angle, she reminded him of Le even more than she had the evening before. She was dressed in a leather miniskirt that reached above the knees, and although from the angle of her head he could not tell if she was wearing makeup, her hair was curled in exactly the same way as his fiancée's. Mr. Tu's heart beat faster as he scurried toward the entrance.

After the movie, Le had insisted on going back alone for some traditional clothes to make it easier for her to blend in with the hordes fleeing the capital. Mrs. Lanh, the madam, was fed up with men and would surely create a scene, she said. She would not be long.

He waited for her on the crowded dock which protruded into the Saigon River at Newport, where the big American ships used to land. Artillery shells pounded the city, and a pall of thick black smoke ringed the metropolis like a funeral wreath. Mr. Tu ran back and forth along the dock, glancing frantically about, mouthing out her name, trying to avoid the bodies trampled in the final rush to freedom and now lying beneath some crude woven mats. He started peeking to see if Le was among them, but stopped when the third body he came to had a face as mutilated as his own. A boat horn blasted behind him. People yelled at him to come on. Slowly, reluctantly, her name still on his lips, with tears struggling to form beneath the dead skin beside his eyelids, he turned away. . . .

———

The librarian date-stamping books behind the checkout desk glared at him as though his face might set off the security alarm, but Mr. Tu glanced only briefly at her as he pushed back the door flap and strode intrepidly toward the stacks. Departing patrons whisked by him, some of them with books crooked under their arms, and paid him hardly any mind. Yet Mr. Tu started to tremble when he saw the row of sunlit windows up ahead and spotted her, poring over her magazine still. Hoa was seated all alone. His feet began to drag, and then he halted in his tracks. The dust particles which danced in the air all along the bookshelf separating them seemed to Mr. Tu's distracted vision to be playing with her hair, which had lightened to a beautiful shade of auburn in the glow of the sun. His mind was in a muddle, and he might have stayed there forever, just watching her, if a young man impatient for a book on the shelf beside him had not roughly ordered him aside. The man was rude, contemptuous, as though Mr. Tu's face gave him the right to be that way. Mr. Tu winced beneath his skin grafts and stepped uncertainly forward.

"Hello," he murmured, coming up to her. He was embarrassed when she didn't hear him. "Hello," he repeated, so loudly this time she jerked her head up from the page.

"Oh, hi," she said mechanically, and Mr. Tu's heart skipped. Didn't she remember who he was? No one could forget a face like his.

"So you come here also," she added, but her tone was flat, devoid of interest. She gazed at a bookshelf behind him. Mr. Tu knew he should leap at the opening which lay before him like a dropped handkerchief in the movies, but just at that moment his Adam's apple snarled up his windpipe and his courage ebbed. After another second the girl lowered her eyes again. She flipped the magazine page, and Mr. Tu heard the paper snap as if she was angry at it.

He shifted awkwardly on his feet. Now that he was standing over her, he didn't have the slightest idea what to say. Hoa remained silent.

"May I join you?" he asked at last, indicating a chair across from her. She flicked her hand, impatiently it seemed, and Mr. Tu settled in and tried to make himself comfortable. But instead he became quite nervous as he stared at the beautiful bowed head and the tantalizing body opposite him, which had stiffened since he sat down. Occasionally she glanced up at the bookshelf again, but not at him. Mr. Tu started to sweat, and the thought that she might smell him filled him with horror. His mouth went dry, and what finally emerged from his throat was little more than a croak.

"Aren't you glad to see me, Miss Hoa?"

She looked at him and smiled slightly, for the first time. Mr. Tu was encouraged.

"Oh, you remembered my name."

"How could I forget it?" he blurted out.

Her face revealed her annoyance, and Mr. Tu's hand twitched spasmodically on his chair arm. He was going too fast. She was trying to sort out her feelings for him, and he had to proceed cautiously.

"I work with flowers, remember," he added, trying to sound casual.

"Ah, yes. So you do." But she merely looked down once more.

Mr. Tu decided to hazard a smile, but stopped midway, afraid his defective face muscles might turn it into a sneer. For a moment he almost envied his father's fate. No one had been indifferent to the little pile of dust which was heaped up in the middle of the old man's rice field and which was virtually indistinguishable from the powdered fertilizer that USAID had given him to increase his crop yield. The farmer's remains were the talk of Long Dien village for weeks.

The sound of raucous laughter suddenly came from behind the bookshelves, and Hoa popped her head up and frowned in its direction. The laughter was followed by giggling, then the hurried whisper of voices, one male, one female. Hoa looked across at Mr. Tu, visibly upset. He summoned up all his courage and flashed her the most engaging smile of which his blackened lips were capable. His smiles had cheered Le through many a troubled time. Hoa trembled slightly, and Mr. Tu felt emboldened. But his skin crinkled like a strip of tanning leather when he spoke again.

"Would you like to get a coffee somewhere?" he squeaked. He sank back down, embarrassed.

She blenched as though someone had yanked a rope around her neck.

"With *you?*" she said, her voice barely above a whisper.

She quickly shook her head, but Mr. Tu did not lose heart. He'd picked up the breathlessness of her reply, the rapid twittering of her fingers on the page. Women were programmed to demur, then to yield. He waited.

"I can't," she said, glancing anxiously at the bookshelves yet again.

Mr. Tu waved his hand as though her refusal was only to be expected. He tried to fix her with his eyes, those beautiful unscarred eyes which the gods had spared from the napalm at An Loc. Le had melted at the sight of them.

"Well," he said, attempting to keep his voice steady, "the Stockade Diner's just up the street."

She peered at him.

"But you're so . . . different," she said.

Mr. Tu's heart withered within him. He thought of Mrs. Hai-li, who never looked him straight on, as though his face might blind her like a solar eclipse.

"You think I'm ugly, don't you?" he said feebly, unable to look at *her* now. He felt as insignificant as a mound of dust.

The laughter resumed behind the bookshelves. Hoa abruptly shut her magazine, and Mr. Tu lifted his head. The girl darted to her feet and moved away from him.

"You're *Vietnamese*," she said, her voice filled with sudden scorn. Her eyes focused on the bookshelves. Mr. Tu's jaw dropped as far as it could.

"But . . . so are *you*," he stammered, his face contorting itself into something resembling a look of perplexity.

She glared back at him and shook her head vehemently.

"That was before," she said. "I want to forget all about that now, and you remind me of—"

A rustling came from the stacks, and Hoa paused in midsentence. Mr. Tu felt angry and hurt. He shot to his feet.

"Of *what?*" he said, his voice rising. He tried to grab her hand, but she drew away from him. "What do I remind you of?"

She didn't answer, for just at that moment Phil emerged from behind the bookshelf. Mr. Tu turned and noticed a wisp of red hair disappear in the direction of the checkout counter. Hoa flitted to the American's side. She scowled distrustfully at him and peered in the direction of the exit. Phil grasped her roughly by the arm and twisted her around.

"Ow!" she yelped, trying to disengage herself. "You're hurting me!"

In spite of her curious remarks to him, Mr. Tu stepped gallantly forward. Only her own people could help her in such a predicament.

"Be gentle with her, young man," he admonished, wagging a stern finger at the American.

Phil stared at him and then gaped at Hoa.

"What the fuck is this bird talking about?" he demanded. All of a sudden, Hoa wrenched free from him and turned on Mr. Tu.

"This is *our* business, so stay out of it!" she yelled. "And yes, you're right. You *are* ugly," she added savagely. "I would never go out with *you!*"

Mr. Tu was astounded. Never had Le treated him like this, nor any of the other ladies who had swooned over him in his youth. He drew himself up proudly in front of her.

"And I would never be seen with a whore like *you*, either!" he cried, tossing his head self-righteously and twisting his face into what he truly intended to be a sneer this time.

Hoa turned white and trembled all over. In a single bound she sprang to Mr. Tu, raised her hand, and slapped him hard across the face. Mr. Tu's skin smarted as though it had been set on fire a second time. He felt dizzy, disoriented, and the tears which had been so many years in coming finally burst from his eyes. In his blindness and confusion the angry young woman with her fist still raised looked as though she stood at the edge of another world, beckoning for him to come back to her. Mr. Tu stretched his hand out and tried to call her name, but no sound emerged from his throat. He staggered against the chair he'd been sitting in and gingerly lowered himself into it. He bowed his head to calm his nerves. When he looked up again, a minute later, he was alone.

Mr. Tu's heart felt as thick and heavy as lead. His face burned fiercely still, and the pain, as it settled deep inside him, was much more intense than it had been the first time, when all he had lost was a battle. A librarian began to switch off the lights in the stacks. She saw Mr. Tu and started. Slowly he rose from his chair.

six

NUMBERS

———————

Thi Hanh and I moved to Tan Chau village last year. Tan Chau lies on the Thanh Hoa canal, which sings with freedom as it flows into the Mekong River on its way to the sea. Only the wind and the water, which you cannot imprison, are truly free. Even Thi Hanh, my daughter once, is no longer free. Children taken by the wood nymphs never are.

I live alone now. In a one-room hut that squats like a huge thatched toad along the canal, surrounded by mangrove swamps, cypresses, and cashew trees. My hut is very small. An oaken cot, an unvarnished pine wood table, a kerosene lamp, a stove, and three chairs. In the evenings, when you should not go out, I sit by my door, running my hands along the scraggly surface of the table as though stroking a salamander, and I wait for the return of Thi Hanh. Finches chirp in a nearby custard apple tree, and grasshoppers ratchet in the hay fields. The monsoons have ceased, and the wet hay smells like the warm matted hair of a water sprite who has surfaced in the canal now that the storm has passed. You say the waters have no spirits? Ask the peasants. In Viet Nam such things are "standard operating procedure," as the Americans say.

These Americans have many little expressions that stick in the mind. I like that, though my native language is French. Are you surprised that Nguyen Minh Long, Third Chief Assessor (Retired) in the Materials Division, Ministry of War, Republic of Viet Nam, speaks French better than Vietnamese? My enemies, Mr. Loc and Miss Huyen, said the only Vietnamese part of me was my "hide," that anybody who came through the French schools like Lasan Taberd was a plant dying of thirst, whose roots never sprouted in native soil and had to turn back to the surface to survive. And their ill will was not confined to *me*. . . .

My hut measures five hundred and seventy-six square feet, exactly. You see I am precise with numbers. I cannot give up old habits easily. When I was an accountant back in Saigon, my numbers were important. Indeed I may say in all modesty that the great success which the Republic of Viet Nam enjoys against the Communist aggressors from the North is due in no small part to the numbers of Nguyen Minh Long. Does that surprise you? Do I strike you, in my seclusion here, as a cog in the wheel? Look at the great river which flows near my village. Is it not made up of billions of tiny drops, each one necessary for reaching the sea? And did not Colonel Dinh, my boss, and even the minister himself once, the Honorable Do Muoi, praise my work?

I remember the day well. Mr. Muoi was on an inspection tour shortly before the 1971 presidential elections. I can be precise, of course. It was at 3:03 p.m. on Monday, September 27, and I had just returned to the Ministry from my afternoon siesta. Shirkers like Mr. Loc and Miss Huyen cheat the government of their time, but I am always back at my desk by 3:00 p.m. sharp. Light streamed through the high arched windows of the central accounting room. They'd just switched on the ceiling fans after the lunch break, and waves of heat coiled up from the floor like charmed cobras. The air was thick with the fumes of petrol from the courtyard where I'd parked my Vespa motorbike. It was very hot and I felt a bit queasy, but I was already bent over my numbers, working hard as usual.

The minister's visit was a momentous event. The election was less than a week away, and our careers depended on a "certain result." The Americans had made it clear that the amount of their aid, a certain number, depended on President Thieu's getting a fixed percentage of the vote, another certain number. Our great leader's victory on October 3 in turn depended on convincing the people he had achieved such and such a level of success against the Communists, other certain numbers. Numbers. The Americans are in love with them. I leave the "body counts" to them. Such things are too crude for me. But Nguyen Minh Long is the master of other numbers, and everyone at the ministry knows that.

That is why Colonel Dinh steered Mr. Muoi straight to my desk that day. The minister peeked over my shoulder, to see I was doing my job as well as he'd been led to expect, I suppose, and all eyes turned toward us. Loc's, particularly, glittered with envy. I was not nervous at all, I remember, even when Mr. Muoi asked me in a commanding voice for the exact number of North Vietnamese tanks sighted in Chau Doc the previous month. Though I knew how important my answer was, I barely glanced at my numbers. They wouldn't have helped anyway, since they are four months behind. But Chau Doc was a troubled region, so I kept the figure low. I told him ten, and the minister broke into a broad smile and clapped me on the back.

"Excellent, Desk No.—"

He looked about for the number, which is tacked on the side.

"Thirteen, Mr. Minister," Colonel Dinh spoke up. "This is Mr. Long, our efficient Third Chief Assessor."

"*Excellent*, Mr. Long," Minister Muoi repeated. "Keep up the good work."

I bowed, for I am a modest man. Mr. Muoi turned to go, explaining he was quite busy just then, caught up in the details of the election, and couldn't stay any longer. But the precise number of North Vietnamese tanks sighted in Chau Doc province in August was fixed forever in his mind. After that can you say Nguyen Minh Long is a mere cog in the wheel?

———

It was not for any little inaccuracies in my reports that I was asked to leave the ministry the next year. Even though Mr. Loc, who coveted my job, and Miss Huyen, whose advances I spurned, spread the rumor that people died because of my numbers. That is the kind of spiteful talk a man like me has to put up with. Is Nguyen Minh Long responsible for the ambush of a regiment in Tay Ninh in June of 1972? Or the hasty retreat from the Central Highlands of General Truong's troops a month later? I am a statistician, not a tactician. My numbers never lie. Colonel Dinh knows that, and put me in for promotion to Second Chief Assessor even as the helicopters flew back from Kontum. Surely *he* would have told me had I been at fault. . . .

No, other rumors, equally false and malicious, forced me to retire. My enemies accused Thi Hanh of keeping company with spirits. "Possessed," I think the term is. They did not call them "spirits" exactly, but I knew what they meant. They said she once stared into the beating heart of a charcoal basket fire at a meatball vendor's and read in the pulsating coals the name of a man doomed to die that night. Tran Van Be. And that she discovered the name of another victim, Nguyen Thai Vinh, by groping inside the torso of a decapitated pheasant at the Marche Central and yanking out the liver, whose texture she then read with her fingers, like the blind. And sure enough, the next day's newspapers carried the obituaries of Tran Van Be and Nguyen Thai Vinh. . . . Or so they said.

I was above such talk, but you will quickly believe how Mr. Loc and Miss Huyen used these preposterous tales to discredit me. *Long's got a mad one in the family. Probably in the blood.*

That kind of talk was mainly Loc's. Huyen was still trying to get me to notice her, sidling by my desk every morning with her *ao dai* slit higher than usual, displaying a thin square of thigh flesh soft and pink as a newborn pig's. . . . But after I "turned a cold shoulder on her," she began to suggest things worse than spirits, that perhaps Third Assessor Long's daughter was not really mad and that something more sinister was behind all those sudden deaths. . . .

As for Hanh herself, of course there was nothing wrong. Nothing at all. It's true I didn't see her much after she started night classes at Van Hanh University, and that we hardly spoke after her mother died in a cross fire during the Tet offensive in 1968. She felt I had no business being away when the Communists attacked, that I must have known something was up. I reminded her that Colonel Dinh had ordered me to Dalat after I suggested I check in person on the numbers I was getting from the Highlands. But when Hanh gets like that, she is as unreasonable as Loc or Huyen, so I have always been closer to her brothers, Cuu and Truyen. You must not misunderstand me. Of course Thi Hanh and I love each other. All children love their parents. But a man is closer to his sons. Still, all this talk about possession was ridiculous.

But once a successful man arouses the envy of his associates, they will stop at nothing to destroy him. About a month before my strange talk with Colonel Dinh, my young assistant Thanh, who worships me, told me people in the office were discussing how "remarkable" it was that the combat units of Nguyen Minh Cuu and Nguyen Minh Truyen never did much fighting, that they always ended up assigned to places like Bien Hoa or Vung Tau.

"They say it's not mere coincidence, Mr. Assessor," Thanh whispered, confidentially. He glanced over his shoulder, and I knew at whom.

"That is outrageous," I replied, though secretly flattered to think Loc and Huyen believed I had the power to influence troop assignments like that. "Scurrilous!"

"They even say," Thanh went on, "that the Fifteenth Division . . ."

He stopped and looked flustered. The Fifteenth Light Armored Division is Cuu's. I bristled.

"They say *what*, Mr. Thanh?" I snapped.

"Well . . . ," Thanh hesitated, glancing back again, "they say—"

"Why do you keep looking over your shoulder? Come on. Out with it."

"Well, Chief Assessor." I like it when Thanh calls me that, and I bowed.

"Well what?"

"They say the Fifteenth is afraid to fight and stays in Vung Tau because it knows the Communists will never attack the coastal resorts."

"What!" I shot up from my desk but quickly remembered what I owed to my position. I glared in the direction of Loc and Huyen, then eased back into my chair.

"*Thank* you, Mr. Thanh," I said loftily, grabbing a paper and pretending I didn't have time for such nonsense. "But you must not believe everything you hear."

I dismissed him with a turn to my numbers. It is not wise to encourage subordinates in this kind of talk. As for Loc and Huyen, for the time being I would do nothing. We have a saying that it is beneath the dignity of the buffalo to swat at flies. I could deal with *them* later.

———

A monsoon breeze fans the palm trees lined like sentries along Pasteur Street. Past old French villas dark and silent in the predawn, swirling among the fronds, twisting in and out of trunks and over and around walls, mindless of the curfew it ignores with impunity. Seven spirits of the night, out following the breeze, also have no curfew. Carrying things as material as ropes and grappling hooks, they vault the wall at No. 217 along with the wind and drop down on the courtyard on the other side. Even spirits divide by gender, and four male and three female, young, permeate stone and darkness unsensed by man or animal. They bend their attention on a certain window on the second floor just off a balcony festooned with wrought-iron lilies. Up from the courtyard clambers a female spirit, lightest and most determined of the seven. She is level with the balcony, black against the night, her face that appears human in the moonlight the only white showing. Her gloved hands clutch the lilies in quest of a grip, and then the slim figure hoists itself over the balcony and down onto the tiles.

Tall frosted windows yawn into the breeze. The spirit penetrates a sitting room, deserted of occupants, the sleeping chamber lying beyond. Tables, credenza, chairs, foils to the material melt in front of her, for the plan of the house was given her several days before. She is not new at this job, is good at it. The distant streetlight at the corner of Pasteur and Phan Dinh Phung streets, more than the dull moon which glances off the cream-colored door of the bedroom, uncovers the bright steel knife which she slides up from her ankle into her hand. Past the door two figures sleep, Vice Minister Bao of the Ministry of Interior and his wife, and the spirit approaches the bed. Silently. One black gloved hand muffles the mouth of Vice Minister Bao and the steel pares the throat at the same time, whipsawing flesh and muscle in a single swift motion with which the young spirit dices life. Vice Minister Bao cannot cry out as his vocal cords snap like strands of cuttlefish and he begins to thrash and drown in the blood of his severed carotid. But in his final minute he opens his eyes and sees, staring back at him, eyes as human as his, round and gray, silent and filled with hate. The spirit takes the hand which wielded the knife and covers the man's eyes as well as his mouth. She leans heavily upon him to squeeze out the last ounce of life. There is not throat enough left for a rattle, only blood everywhere, which wets and threatens to rouse the wife now tossing on the other side of the bed. The spirit grips the knife again and hurries round, but the woman,

though awake at last, is easier to kill. She lies without a sound,
eyes open, yielding and unbelieving, not that she is about to die
but that it is another woman who has come to do this job of
killing. She collapses under the knife, and the spirit, her task
completed, removes her blood-soaked gloves and pins a paper
to the pillow. A political tract, a warning to the finders in the
morning, much like those she has left behind on other beds, and
then she leaves.

———

"We do not question your loyalty, Mr. Long. It's just that your family seems—well, so peculiarly situated."

"How so, my colonel?"

Nguyen Minh Long always speaks in a respectful but dignified tone to his superiors. Even when what they have to convey is unpleasant. I could never have risen to the rank of Third Chief Assessor without knowing my place. I attempted a smile and nodded slightly at Colonel Dinh's use of the word "peculiarly."

"Consider what is said of your sons," he went on, looking up from his desk. "Your older one doesn't seem to do much, does he?"

I knew this was coming, of course, from what Thanh had told me, and I arched my back for battle. The ceiling fan chopped the air overhead, and fine eddies of wind whirled round me like the harpies of slander let loose by Loc and Huyen. I fixed the colonel with my eye, for I had my reputation and that of my family to maintain.

"Cuu is with his unit at Vung Tau," I said. "He does what his commander tells him."

Colonel Dinh planted his elbows on the desk in a triangle ending with his fingertips, as though he were praying. The nails were dirty, as always, but I had never fully noticed them before. The colonel had a farmer's nails. *Nha que* nails. I looked down at my own hands, which Madame Sanh at the Eden Roc had worked so hard over just the day before. They were so silken, so smooth. I glanced up again. *Nha que*. It is not a term of respect in my country. Far from it.

"I would hope so, Mr. Long," he said, a bit sternly to my thinking. "But that is not the point. The whole unit is idle because they have not been ordered to the field."

Colonel Dinh paused and leaned back in his chair. I kept my eyes steady on him, for Nguyen Minh Long has nothing to fear. I was determined to force him to finish the thought with no help from me.

"Even though the Twelfth and Eighteenth regiments of the North Vietnamese Third Division have been spotted just north of Phuoc Le in recent days. Here—"

He leaned forward and reached inside a drawer.

"—look at these. They were taken just last week."

He handed me some reconnaissance photos. I vaguely remember seeing a tank or two, and some missiles. Such things were not new to me. I handed them back in silence, making sure I did not come in contact with those dirty nails.

"Well?" he said, his voice rising. "Why this NVA activity not report? What you say about that?"

I winced. Whenever Colonel Dinh gets excited, he drops his words. It is distressing for an educated man to listen to. *Nha que, nha que*, I kept thinking, like a mantra I couldn't dislodge from my head. If only he'd gone to the Lycee. . . .

"These photos could be taken anywhere." I tried to remain deferential. "As for the regiments, you said yourself they'd only been spotted *recently*." I applauded myself on my reasoning. "How could I incorporate them into my analysis yet?"

Colonel Dinh, though an adequate *fonctionnaire*, is not bright, and what I said made him hesitate. I smiled indulgently. I like the French word for bureaucrat. It expresses the mediocrity of individuals like Colonel Dinh with dirty fingernails exactly. Capable of functioning. Nothing more.

"Well then, what about your other son? Truyen. What do you say about him?"

"What about him?" I shot back, with perhaps not quite the unction he expected. He seemed taken aback.

"Are you aware that he has deserted his platoon? In fact, seven months ago."

Vindictive persons like Loc and Huyen might have said I blanched at this startling accusation, but they would be wrong. Nguyen Minh Long has always been remarkably self-possessed.

"That cannot *be*, my colonel," I responded, though not as quickly as I might have.

"And that you have always reported his unit at Bien Hoa to be intact?" he pursued. He now stood up and placed his arms straight downward on the desk, leaning forward toward me. I peered at his hands, searching for the dirty fingernails, but all I could see were his fists on the desk, knuckles outward. Somehow this disarranged me.

"Well, I . . ." I hesitated.

"You what?" Colonel Dinh snapped. He positively *snapped*, of that I am certain. It was *my* turn to be taken aback.

"Well, I . . . , I don't know," I said. The Americans would have said I "hemmed and hawed." I could hardly look at him. "That was the way it was reported to me."

"Then how do you explain *this?*" Colonel Dinh reached inside his desk again and pulled out a document which he thrust at me. *Report on Nguyen Minh Truyen, Private First Class, Twenty-third Airborne Division, Army of the Republic of Viet Nam, Bien Hoa, Viet Nam.* And the date, some five months earlier. My eyes did not go past the fateful word "AWOL." I felt faint and handed the paper back to him, saying, "But this is the first I have heard of this. Surely you do not believe that *I*, Nguyen Minh Long, would deliberately falsify military records? Who says this of me?"

Although I knew. Colonel Dinh just stared at me in silence.

"I really know nothing of this, my colonel. You must believe me," I said, although, even to my way of thinking, without much conviction.

"That's what you say," he said disdainfully, stuffing the document back into his drawer. "But now," he added, smiling smugly and sitting down again, "tell me about your daughter."

Before long they will make me chief here, in Tan Chau village. I am sure of that. I can see how they look up to me. Even though those little rumors about Thi Hanh forced me from the ministry. These people know nothing about that, of course, and besides, they need organization, someone who has a sense of government. And well, to put it modestly, someone with talent, too.

I wonder whether Thi Hanh will come back to watch my return to power. I hope so. Though she was always different when she was young—stern, silent for days, wandering off by herself even at the strangest hours. The Tan Dinh night guard brought her home once after curfew, saying they didn't have the heart to throw her into Chi Hoa prison, she was that pretty. . . . Think of what Miss Huyen would have made of *that*. A daughter of Third Chief Assessor Long in jail! Thi Hanh wouldn't tell me where she'd been that night, even after I beat her. . . .

And now she has gone off with the wood nymphs, with the spirits. I miss her, of course, the way all parents miss a child who has failed to understand them. There is a sense of incompleteness, of something that needs to be "wrapped up" between us. Even when Thi Hanh was still here, our life together was . . . inconclusive. And now she has gone.

In the afternoons, before the rains come, I sit on a little campstool on my verandah and stare at the black waters of the canal as they crawl past my hut, and I wait for her return. A dry wind furls the channel and lifts the sweet sugary scent of ripening cassava from the manioc field and sets it down at my door. You can almost feel the leaven thickening in the air. Otherwise the forests, the fields, are stagnant and still. It is as though the earth itself is waiting for Thi Hanh. Tinselled dragonflies skim the duckweed-choked canal, their laced wings crackling like electric filament as they hunt for mosquitoes. Every so often a huge dragonfly swoops down on an insect hiding behind a lily pad and tears it free, soaring off again without getting a wing wet. It is amazing. I love to watch them, for hours sometimes, preying on the life beneath them. . . . They say Nguyen Van Phuan, the village chief in Cho Moi, twenty miles downriver, tried to hide too, just like those mosquitoes, with no more success. . . . It makes me pause when I think of my plans here, but Phuan was not particularly smart.

You don't believe in wood nymphs? Before what happened to Thi Hanh I would have agreed with you, calling them a peasant superstition which a sophisticated man should laugh at. But now I am not so sure. Nguyen Minh Long is Vietnamese, after all, and these beliefs run deep among my people. In fact, we have a whole world of spirits here, who inhabit the thin gray line between the real and the unreal like ghostly sentinels of the crepuscule. Spirits of the woods, the lakes and rivers, the sky and earth. I have never seen one myself. I am not susceptible to such things. But Mother Quy, the old woman in the hut next to mine, swears she saw the wood nymphs that took away Thi Hanh.

My daughter had gone out walking to the end of the village, just as the sun was setting, as was her custom. I often warned her not to. We have no curfew here, but we have the fear of the Communists to keep us inside when night falls. But even in this, to my great disappointment, Thi Hanh would not listen to me.

On that night Ba Quy was out late herself, doing her washing in the canal because her brother Ngai was expected from Rach Gia the next day. As it was getting dark and she was bending over in the water, scrubbing the wet sheets with pumice stone and humming a folk tune to ward off evil spirits, she sensed something behind her and wheeled, frightened out of her wits. But it was only Thi Hanh, dressed all in black. She was walking in a trance, Ba Quy says, pale as the moon goddess. Mother Quy called out good evening, but Thi Hanh passed her by without a word. She just kept marching toward the bamboo forest at the edge of the village. Feeling slighted, and not a little curious, Ba Quy stumbled along the bank behind her, keeping in the shadows. Then she saw them. Three or four black figures sprang up out of the earth and swallowed Thi Hanh the way my dragonflies gobble their prey. Ba Quy leaped back when she saw them and stifled a cry, or they would have swallowed her, too. For a moment she took them to be human, for they murmured something to Thi Hanh, who appeared to answer. But when my child disappeared into the earth with them, Ba Quy screamed and ran in terror, back along the canal straight to her hut, where she clapped the door shut and lay shivering in the dark the rest of the night. She even forgot her laundry, which her neighbors found floating in the water the next day.

Mother Quy is certain it was the wood nymphs, even though her eyes are bad and it was late. She insists Thi Hanh would not have followed them into the earth without resisting if they had been anything else. They must have bewitched her. And it was the ease with which Thi Hanh slipped into the supernatural that caused the old woman to panic and run away. . . .

Ba Quy says she is gone forever, that once a person is taken by the wood nymphs she never returns to the land of the living. But I have my doubts. Such things are too absurd, really, and besides, I want my daughter to witness my return to public life. That is why I sit here, day after day, on my campstool at the edge of the canal, thinking not so much of my enemies' victory over me back in Saigon as of my great plans for Tan Chau. You see, Nguyen Minh Long is an optimist. And I watch my dragonflies circle and swoop down on the mosquitoes below, who have no inkling of the fate hovering over them. As for my daughter, Thi Hanh, I know she will return.

seven

UNDER THE RATTAN STICK

The blood started running again in streaks down his back. At dawn on the morning of Monday, March 30, 1891, it woke him, just as though he was in the throes of a fever sweat. Pham the Malabar carriage driver wanted to cry out like a humiliated child wetting his bed at the sticky feel of the mattress, the sickening smell, as the coarse jute fibers which had started it flowing dug into his skin like hungry bull ants. He shuddered, sat up, and drew in great gulps of air steeped in the warm tropical night. Then he realized that the bed was dry, as was his back, and that he'd imagined the whole thing. He flushed at the unfortunate nightmare. On the cot next to him Luong awoke. He shifted and gazed across at Pham.

"What is it?" Luong's voice pierced the quiet. "Pham? Are you all right?"

A stonechat twittered in the cajuput tree just outside the dormitory window, as if it was nervous about the coming day. Down the long row of bunks, the rickshaw porters, landau and hackney drivers, hostlers, and stable boys shifted also, in their sleep, as though Luong had started a wave. They unloosed the scent of hay and horse dung, the smell of the newly-laid macadam of the Boulevard Bonard and of the tamarind, mulberry, and oleander leaves which clogged the city streets. And the stench of unwashed bodies forced to work eighteen-hour days in the blistering Saigon sun.

Pham read the worry which flickered in Luong's eyes, but he gestured impatiently at his comrade's concern. "Get up," he said sternly.

Blue veins of smoke still spiralled upward from the night lamp above the window at the end of the row, but the sun already rose out of the Saigon River just beyond, red as an open wound. Pham prodded Luong with his carriage whip. "You have to create a diversion tonight when you see the coaches coming. Can you do it?"

Luong swung his legs over and sat up. "What . . . what if they *see* me?" His voice wobbled with misgiving.

The other men rubbed their eyes as the blood leached out of the sun and blinded them awake. Pham gave Luong's wrist an encouraging squeeze. The bones felt as brittle as a bird's.

"It's only for a moment," he said. He leaned close, notwithstanding the smell of caked-on sweat which cloaked Luong from head to foot.

"This state visit has set the authorities on edge and made them overly cautious," Pham whispered. "We must distract them. I'll show you where later. But will you do it?"

Luong's body went taut. He looked as though he was afraid to even blink. He dried his hands on his cot, but perspiration soon sprouted on the palms again. His only answer was an uncertain nod, but for Pham it was enough.

———

The trip had been planned for months, in Krasnoye Selo, and Nikolai was looking forward to it. The gloom that had visited him ten years earlier, when his grandfather, Alexander II, was assassinated, had settled in again. Along with the fear, thick and choking as the smoke which rose from ten thousand Petersburg chimneys and half as many street fires, a few scraps of coal mostly, in the latter case, pinched from supply carts or filched outright from the back of the army mess hall on Vozdesvensky Street. Narodnya Volya, the People's Will, had been snuffed out for good, but others had risen to take the place of Grandfather's murderers. The streets bred them faster than the Okhrana could eliminate them.

Nikolai used to drive those streets in his droshky, showering the crowds which came to watch him with Alexander Nevsky kopeks. The shiny silver coins glittered like radiant moons in the scabrous palms of the workmen, and Nikolai hoped the hawk-like brow and truncheon jaw of the great warrior who'd repelled the Swedes and the Teutons would inspire them with renewed love for Russia, for himself. But their faces had turned sulky lately, their mouths muttered only resentful thanks, and he no longer rode out among them.

His father, Alexander III, had wanted him to see the world, and so the three frigates had set out from Gatschina on October 23 of the preceding year. The Successor to the Throne strolled the quarterdeck of the flagship, the "Pamjat Asowa," in his favorite uniform, Battalion Commander of the Preobrazhensky Regiment, the Cross of St. David pinned to his chest, and his heart beat high with anticipation. The East, with its dangers and possibilities, excited him beyond words. And every league that separated him from the capital lightened his mind of the weight of the revolutionaries brooding in the streets behind him. . . .

Pham set off at a brisk pace along the South Fort Road, Luong at his side. Together they sprang across the newly built swing bridge onto the commercial side of the quay, where the odor of fertilizer from the warehouses, Indian spices and anchovies from the ships unloading at the Messageries Maritimes dock, and cattle and poultry from the native sampans bound for the slaughterhouses further up the canal, gave way to softer, more refined smells, more European. Pham's teeth worked like pincers in his jaw as he wound his way through a crowd of white-suited French *colons* waiting outside the shuttered gate of the Banque de l'Indochine on the Quai Belgique. Plantation owners, rubber, tea, and coffee. The smell of their rich cologne, their starched collars, the fresh leather of their boots, rankled in his heart. A black-frocked man with a white ruffle came to open the bank gate, and the planter nearest the Malabar driver waved his hand in the air and called out to him. In his upraised fist he clutched a great wad of piasters. Pham turned pale when he saw it, and his eyes narrowed into little slits of hatred. Blood money, every bill of which had been taken out on the back of a Vietnamese. He stalked away and left Luong behind. . . .

―――――

Four years earlier Pham was working one of the big Engleberg hullers at the Bo Lien rice factory on the Quai des Jonques. He went by another name then, supplied him by the People's Resistance Committee for the Saigon-Gia Dinh region. One day the factory supervisor, Phat Lao, came in with a huge French gypsy with a bulging nose. The bullet-headed giant beat a rattan stick reinforced with steel wires against his side.

"You!" Phat Lao yelled. "Come down here!"

Pham did not move. His hands trembled as he poured a 50-kilo bag of paddy down the Engleberg's chute, and rice grains clicked and scattered like mah jongg tiles on the aluminum floor of the platform on which he stood. The fragrance of rice talc wafted like a balm from the far side of the winnower, but Pham's temples throbbed with dread. He stared at the rest of the rice as it shuttled through the rubber rollers beneath him on its way to the blowers and the German winnowing sieve, as though his very life depended on staying exactly where he was. Phat Lao took a paper from his pocket.

"You see *this?*" he shouted. Pham seized up at the sight of it. "Come down here, I say, or I'll send this one up after you." Phat Lao indicated the big thug. The gypsy smacked his stick against his side again and smiled wickedly.

Pham flipped the control button to the off position. The Engleberg shuddered for a second and then wheezed to a halt. With his other hand he shoved the rest of the flyers he'd printed up the night before, in the basement of one of the committee's safe houses in Cholon, deeper into his pocket. His foot shook terribly as he turned and placed it on the top rung of the ladder. . . .

———

Luong caught up with him at the Signal Mast on the Pointe des Blagueurs. Pham stared up at the French tricolor, which flapped in the wind coming off the canal from the top of a 100-foot pole. A group of young Frenchwomen in crinoline talked fervently on the benches which curved around the base of the flagpole. The scent of their perfume rose above the fetid smell of the river at Pham's back. The Malabar driver lowered his eyes and glared at them.

"I hear he is very handsome, *n'est-ce pas?*" one of the women said. "You know, don't you, Gabrielle?"

She turned and playfully squeezed the elbow of the girl beside her. Gabrielle drew a pocket handkerchief from a gem-studded purse and pretended to dab her eyes.

"*Eh bien oui,* my dears"—and she fetched up a sigh which grabbed the attention of all—"and just last night he waltzed so *divinely,* after the performance at the Opera House. What a charmer! And then that Glinka mazurka! But I only got to dance with him twice." Here she pouted.

The breeze caught her handkerchief suddenly, and it flew from her hand and landed at Pham's feet. Gabrielle gave a little shriek.

"Fetch my hankie!" she ordered, when she saw the two poorly-dressed Vietnamese. She huddled against her friends, however, and peered up at the French flag as if for protection. The breeze whipped up again, and the handkerchief began to drift toward the river. "Quickly!"

Pham put his foot down on top of it. The tricolor rustled in the wind, and he gazed up at the flagpole again. The steel shaft flashed in the sunlight like the blade of a sword. In 1883, two Vietnamese were beheaded at the foot of the Signal Mast for assassinating Boileux, the director of the Registration Service. Pham's face darkened. Slowly he began to grind the handkerchief into the pavement.

"What are you *doing?*" Gabrielle gasped. She glanced desperately around. "Help! Someone!" The other girls looked shocked.

Luong nervously nudged his companion.

"Pham, please. We don't want trouble." He turned to the Frenchwomen and gave them an ingratiating smile. Then he bowed, just like the two rebels who'd exposed their necks to execution on the same spot eight years earlier.

"I'm sorry, *Mesdemoiselles,*" he said, in pidgin French. "We didn't mean—"

Pham yanked Luong's head up and shook him by the scruff of the neck.

"*Never* bow to them. Understand?"

He brought his face so close to Luong's that he could feel the heat of his friend's breath. Luong timorously nodded, and Pham released his hold. Gabrielle's hysterical screams rang in their ears as they marched away.

———

First there was Cairo and Memphis, where Nikolai had gazed awestruck at the fallen statue of Ramses II and reflected soberly on the fleeting fortune of rulers. But his spirits soon rebounded, what with all the delightful parties and excursions. The dancing dervishes of Aswan captivated him, as did the sensuous houris of Luxor. How exquisite these creatures were, how eager to please, as they served him olives, pomegranates, and a selection of the finest Nile wines in sparkling gold goblets! Nikolai had visions of the slaves of Cleopatra, from his childhood picture books at Peterhof, and he pulsed with envy. He thought with sorrow of the sullen faces that greeted him everywhere back home now. Here at least they treated him like a king. . . .

He visited the tombs of Apis with his cousin, Prince George of Greece, far from the hand-wringing and caterwauling of the two lynx-eyed advisers his father had set over him, Baratinsky and Bassargin. . . . Only when he was alone with George did he confess how intimidated he was by these crusty veterans of the Crimea, who looked down on him with the dour superciliousness of wet-nurses. The dreary pair dressed in black, like undertakers, and oppressed him terribly. Baratinsky in particular, who was thin and cutting as a razor and had a vulture's beak to boot. . . .

Then came India and Ceylon, the temples of Benares, the farewell illumination in the city of Madura, the Temple of Kandy and the Tooth of Buddha, and, most happily, the long-awaited reunion with Uncle Grand-Duke Alexander Mikhailovich on the yacht "Tamara" on his way back home. No mean veteran himself, Alexander Mikhailovich, his breast sprouting medals like a fecund garden, chilled the caterwaulers with his glassy stare and sent them packing with their tails between their legs. One day he even gave Baratinsky a public dressing-down for referring to the Inheritor of the Throne as a "toy soldier" fit for nothing but a parade. That same "toy soldier" had been sent by his royal father to pull the East into Russia's orbit, Uncle reminded him, supplanting old Europe, and Baratinsky was well advised to remember it! Nikolai rejoiced at the undertaker's comeuppance, and when they set sail again he strode the quarterdeck with a new spring to his step and held his head higher than the mainmast. Baratinsky didn't emerge from his cabin for two whole days. . . .

―――――

The transport ship *Loire* lay at anchor across from them, its deck glittering with whitewash and its gangplanks festooned with bunting in the French and Russian national colors. Hammers rattled noisily in the still morning air, and the smell of fresh varnish drifted across Rigault de Genouilly Square. Pham stepped back into the shade of a *cay bang* tree and kneaded his aching forehead. It was in just such a ship that all the French had arrived, including Phat Lao's big thug. Pham could almost feel his back fire up with pain again, and he lurched against a low-hanging bough as if to escape the gypsy's blows. A couple of *cay bang* leaves fluttered to his feet like disoriented birds. He recovered his equilibrium, tapped Luong on the shoulder, and pointed to the Directorate of Port Movements on the other side of the stele of Doudart de Lagree.

"That's where you should wait. Right behind that big aglaiata."

Luong nodded but didn't say anything.

"You'll be screened from onlookers." Pham tapped him a second time, but his friend's shoulder gave way under his touch. Luong glanced furtively around but avoided Pham's eyes. The Malabar driver let his breath out slowly to keep from showing his annoyance.

"Governor-General Piquet will be in the lead coach, along with the Russian, and I'll be right behind. If you can only get them to stop, just for a few moments, then—"

"Step aside there!"

A Vietnamese worker flew up to them and knelt at their feet. Carefully he attached a brass plaque to the pedestal of the statue of Admiral Genouilly. The plaque depicted the storming of the Saigon citadel by the admiral's forces in February 1859. Another one further down the way showed the arrival of the French fleet at Cap St. Jacques. Pham's irritation increased as he gazed at them.

"What are *those* for?" he asked sharply. The worker glanced up at him in surprise.

"Who wants to know?" he shot back. He stared at their tattered shirts, their filthy shorts, the calluses on their feet. "Why, you're nothing but rickshaw drivers!" His mouth formed a contemptuous grin, which died at the look on Pham's face.

"The royal visitor gave them to Governor-General Piquet," he explained, meekly now. "To celebrate local history. They're supposed to go along with *that* guy." He pointed up at the admiral, who'd completed his conquest of Saigon in the early sixties. Rigault de Genouilly leaned against a gun carriage and peered into the distance as though still seeking out rebels on the other side of the river. Pham imagined the little bearded Russian, whom he'd seen swaggering along the deck of his frigate two days earlier, standing side by side with the French conqueror and nodding in approval at each cannon burst. He bristled with resentment.

"*Whose* history are you talking about?" he snapped. "Not ours."

The workman shifted anxiously on his knees. He looked around.

"You'd better not say that," he whispered. "They've got eyes everywhere. See?" He directed his gaze across the way.

Two gendarmes stood on the quay beneath the transport ship, watching them closely. Behind them a squadron of French sailors carried chairs, tables, even a samovar up the gangplank onto the *Loire*. They were followed by a group of half-naked coolies lugging gifts for the tsarevitch. Trunks inlaid with mother-of-pearl and ivory, some big Japanese bronzes, a couple of cumbersome pieces of Satsuma pottery.... Several of the Vietnamese laborers panted hard as they trudged up the steep incline.

"They probably think you're going to steal that stuff." The workman laughed nervously.

Pham ignored him and kept his eyes trained on the coolies. His heart filled with the bitterness of their degradation. A fragrant pepperwood box clutched by one of them sent its aroma across the square, but the rich pleasant smell only made their plight seem more ignominious. These Vietnamese hunkering under the presents for the tsarevitch looked like pack animals hauling around the entire weight of colonialism on their backs.

Suddenly Pham hated the Russian as much as he despised the man's hosts. He turned away from the transport ship and squared his chest with resolve. He peered at Luong.

"Come. We have work to do."

———

Fontrim, his manservant, had made him lime water and tea, but Nikolai's head still ached as he stood in full dress uniform in the late morning light on the balcony of the Governor-General's palace and looked out over Saigon. Red-tiled roofs poked like islets through a scrim of sea-green foliage. A breeze from the Avalanche Arroyo brought him the breath of an early blooming jackfruit, the hint of hibiscus, and Nikolai thought of his carefree youthful days in the countryside at Tsarskoi Selo, far from the revolutionaries. All night dinner parties, Hungarian wine mulled in samovars, the latest farce of Feydeau or Victorien Sardou, Caucasians dancing the lezginka. . . . And the women! Pirouettes around the ice rink at Anichkovo with one of the Sheremetev girls, the bewitching creature gazing at him with eyes as sweet as honey. Breakneck sleigh rides on the frozen Neva, a stolen kiss or two. . . . How heavenly it all was! Nikolai sighed.

His head began to hurt less, but he now turned grumpy at the memory of the night before. He and George had wanted to sneak off at the end of the reception in the elegant assembly hall, at 3:00 a.m., and find some girls in one of the "bamboo" houses on Admiral Courbet Street, along with the moody Burmese prince, Myn-Goon-Min, who moped about the ballroom in silk robes and a red turban, his fingers bedecked with rings. A pretender to the throne like himself, the prince wandered from place to place, cosseted but kept on a very short leash by his father's advisers, and Nikolai had sympathized with him at once. How the awareness of their deferred power festered inside them both! But Baratinsky and Bassargin had kept their spiders' eyes on them the whole evening, and they could not go out. Another sigh sieved through his lips. . . .

He heard a laugh and gazed down over the circular gravel driveway leading up to the foyer. He spotted a group of bare-headed coolies below him, chained together and filling in a pit with wooden spades. Several French soldiers with rattan sticks stood over them, watching as the last link in the chain shoveled dirt from a narrow-gauge tram car and handed it down the line, where the lead coolie dumped it into the hole, which looked to have been a pond once. The smell of peat rose in the air around the balcony. One of the coolies tripped suddenly and dropped his load of dirt, and a big gendarme was on top of him in an instant. He swore at the poor fellow and beat him furiously with his stick, until the man's back was as red and pulpy as a watermelon. The coolie hollered and dodged about in an effort to escape the blows, but he got snarled in his chains and lay whimpering on the ground until the huge gendarme had spent his rage. Nikolai felt uncomfortable at first, watching them, but several of the other coolies were still laughing, in spite of the beating, and their merriment soon perked him up. The man must have deserved it.

He noticed how hot it was, and stepped back into the cool marble alcove to avoid the heat and forget the distressing scene, which began to bother him again. The scent of potted bougain-villea on either side of him gradually soothed his overwrought spirits. How compliant these coolies were! How had the French managed to reconcile them to their fate? Why couldn't his subjects be that accommodating? He recalled the stream of curses which had vomited from Petrovskaya's mouth at her trial for Grandfather's murder, when she vowed to bring the entire imperial clique to its knees. Nikolai shuddered at the recollection. . . . Outside the rattan stick went to work again, and the coolie resumed his howls. Nikolai decided to stay in the alcove where it was pleasant. . . .

———

Pham tugged the reins, and the little Annamese pony pulling the Malabar carriage turned left onto Norodom Boulevard at the chevet of Notre Dame Cathedral. A string of brightly-colored Chinese lanterns dangled from the candleberry trees on either side of the boulevard like huge lighted leaves, and crowds of Europeans gathered on the sidewalk to watch the magnificent procession of coaches and landaus headed toward the Governor-General's palace. In another hour they would witness the return of the carriages along the same route, and the tsarevitch would take his leave of Saigon at the farewell ball later that evening on board the *Loire*. Perfumed handkerchiefs flew about like scented bugs as each vehicle passed, and bursts of admiration pelted the night air.

"Hurry it on, will you?" Herve de Colombes barked, from the back of the Malabar. "They're waiting for us."

Pham clicked his tongue, and the pony quickened its pace. The springs of the carriage squeaked as Colombes shifted restlessly in his seat, and the smell of newly polished leather drifted into the front. After three years in hiding and a complete change of identity, Pham had managed to secure the position of coachman to the Governor-General's adjutant, and the resistance committee expected great things of him. He felt the bulge in his pocket and smiled to himself as the Malabar carriage swayed from side to side. He would not let them down.

"What's *this*?" the adjutant said after a few minutes, when they suddenly hit a bottleneck. He leaned forward and petulantly slapped the back of Pham's seat.

The carriage halted near the traffic circle in Pellerin Street. Pham heard cries coming from the statue of Gambetta in the middle of the circle.

"How horrible!" a tall Frenchwoman in a long billowing dress said, from the base of the monument to the great reformist statesman. She stared down at something and shielded her face with her hands. Several other Europeans stood by looking on, their faces expressionless. Gambetta gazed out over the boulevard in his fur-lined greatcoat, heedless of the scene beneath him.

"Ooh!" the woman cried, peeking through her fingers. Diamond rings glittered on both hands. "What's he doing *here*?"

"He was working at the Palace and attacked one of the gendarmes, they say," a man beside her explained. "They had to get him out of there before he spoiled the festivities. They left him here to teach the others a lesson."

"Well, they don't have to teach *us* anything!" the woman exclaimed, stomping off. In the space that opened Pham saw the body of a half-naked coolie crumpled at Gambetta's feet. The man's neck was broken, and blood streamed from long scarlet welts down his back. The coolie was caked with dirt and smelled of the earth, and his sweat glistened like a vein of ore. Pham's heart plunged to his stomach as he peered at him.

Herve de Colombes rapped him on the collarbone.

"They're moving again! Hop to it!"

Pham trembled with suppressed rage and savagely yanked the reins. The startled pony whinnied and clopped off. They drove through the high wrought-iron gates into the palace grounds, and the carriage proceeded along the driveway. The marble portico ahead of them was lit up like a Messageries ocean liner. Pham stopped at the bottom of the staircase, and Herve de Colombes jumped out of the carriage and sprinted up the steps. Pham waited fretfully for the hackney coach in front of him to move on. He had to force himself to remain calm.

"My compliments, Excellency," a voice boomed from the center of the porch, in deep rumbling tones. The French was slightly accented. "You did a good job putting down that rebel."

Pham turned his head, and his eyes scanned the portico. *What rebel?* Slowly he set the reins down.

"Alas, if we could only manage them as well back home!" the voice boomed again, this time with a slight chuckle. At that moment the crowd in the middle of the porch parted, and Nikolai stepped forward. His full brown beard and long sleek sideburns shimmered in the light of an overhead chandelier. His chest was covered with medals, every one of which filled Pham with sorrow. *How much blood had been shed to forge them?* he wondered.

"*Merci,* Highness," Governor-General Piquet said, giving Nikolai a bow. His heels clacked smartly on the tiles, and the odor of lilac-scented cologne sprayed across the portico. "You are too kind. These things are unpleasant, however," he added, shaking his head and extending his hand. One fine white kid glove tipped the fingers of the other.

"But necessary, eh?" The tsarevitch gave Piquet a sly wink. "Offer them your finger and they'll take your arm, you know. You have to crush them at every turn."

All eyes were fixed on the imperial visitor and his host, and Pham got out of the carriage unnoticed, his decision suddenly taken. Nikolai's last words pounded in his ears, and his mind burned with fury at the little man. *What right did* he *have to come here and revel in their disgrace?* People clustered around the two dignitaries, straining to get a better glimpse of them. Pham sucked his breath in and crept to the staircase. He thrust his hand in his pocket and placed his foot on the bottom step. He no longer had any need of Luong.

Two black-uniformed old men stood on either side of the royal guest at the top of the staircase, trying to keep the awe-struck crowd away. A musty smell arose from both of them. One of them, a thin, hook-nosed man, noticed Pham. Their eyes locked, and the old man stepped in front of Nikolai and pressed him back from the edge of the porch.

"What is it?" Nikolai cried. His voice had lost its volcanic rumble.

"Make way there!" a voice shouted from the driveway. Everyone looked in its direction, except for Pham and the old Russian. And Nikolai. Pham took his hand out of his pocket. His gaze met the tsarevitch's as the royal visitor peeked around the old man's shoulder to see what had caused the sudden commotion. The Malabar driver scowled at him. Nikolai turned white, and his medals flickered and went out like lights in a storm as he ducked behind his protector again. Pham's lip curled in scorn. His foot found the second step.

"I said, make way!"

A huge gendarme elbowed past Pham and struggled up the stairs. Something wiggled in his arms. The Frenchman wrestled his burden to the ground and rose to his feet. Several people cried out in consternation.

"What is *this?*" M. Piquet demanded, his eyes fixed sternly on the big intruder. The tsarevitch popped his head out from behind his guardian's shoulder a second time.

"Not to worry, Excellencies," the gypsy said, bowing to the Governor-General and Nikolai in turn. "We found this fellow loitering suspiciously down by the *Loire,* and he refused to tell us what he was up to." He whipped out a rattan stick, and Pham froze as the steel wires he remembered so well flashed before him. "But we'll have it out of him in a jiffy!" The stick came down with a loud crack on Luong's shoulder blade.

"Ow!" Luong yelped, writhing in pain. "Please!" But the gypsy's arm flew up and down like lightning. His victim moaned desolately. Pham climbed the third step, his jaw hardened into flint. The hook-nosed Russian loomed above him, barring his way. His eyes shone fiercely.

"Don't leave me!" Nikolai exclaimed, still in French. "Baratinsky!"

The old man hesitated. Pham was astonished to see a look of contempt on his face which mirrored his own. Luong whimpered on the floor still, and Nikolai's guardian moved aside. Once more the gendarme started to raise his arm, exposing the vital organs. The crowd stared at him, transfixed, and awaited the next blow. Pham bounded up the last step with the swiftness of a civet cat. The old man watched him intently but did nothing to stop him. Nikolai clung to his protector's greatcoat. Pham plunged his hand into his pocket again, and his eyes homed in on the gigantic back in front of him. He stepped forward. The others could wait.

eight

BROTHER DANIEL'S ROSES

Brother Daniel Nguyen looked up from his grading and peered over the top of his horn-rimmed glasses at the approach of his niece. Kim Hong was dressed in blue jeans and a light pink blouse, much to his annoyance. A whiff of hyacinth perfume preceded her entrance into his little cell, one of about forty ranged in a square around the courtyard of Lasan Taberd High School in downtown Saigon. The noise of the incessant traffic outside on Nguyen Du Street, the buses and motorbikes, the black Citroen 15 CV taxicabs, even the loud and smoky American military vehicles, disturbed him far less than the appearance of the seventeen-year-old girl who stepped across the threshold. "Hong" in Vietnamese signified the rose, and there was a self-conscious blush on her cheek which fully justified her name. Frère Daniel cultivated roses. He now glanced down at the paper beneath his eyes, and with a quick jab of the pen wrote "Unacceptable" across it. Then he stared up at her.

"Where were you last night?"

Kim Hong flinched at his tone. Thunder began to roll in from the south, across the Saigon River, and a sharp breeze ruffled the leaves of the large kapok tree in the middle of the courtyard. It was the beginning of April, 1967, and the monsoon season had started early. Two of the other Vietnamese brothers, Frères Sebastien Trung and Khach Viviani, bolted past the kapok in search of shelter, the tails of their cassocks whipped up by the strong wind. Kim Hong gazed uneasily at her uncle. The smell of approaching rain hung in the air between them.

"Why, at home, Uncle, of course." But she peeped down at the floor. The room became dark suddenly and heated like an oven, and the fluorescent lamp on the wall behind Daniel's desk sputtered as it did every afternoon right before the deluge. Drops of perspiration broke out on the cleric's brow, and when Kim Hong glanced up again, she looked as though she was afraid that she, too, might begin to sweat. Frère Daniel rose to his feet and came around the desk.

"You were at Brodard's, weren't you? You were seen."

Her blush deepened as she stepped back from him.

"*Who* saw me?" she demanded. "They have no right." She lowered her head a second time when her uncle gave no response. "I was with friends," she muttered.

"But *he* was there, wasn't he?"

Kim Hong edged back another pace.

"Wasn't he?"

She peered up at him at last.

"But he was not with us, Uncle. It was a coincidence. We went there for *une glace à la fraise*, and he was eating dinner by himself. How could we know he'd be there?"

The bronzed French clock on top of the PTT building on the other side of Nguyen Du Street struck the hour, and just as though it was on a timer the downpour began, in a torrent that would soon shift into a steady drumbeat which would last until dark. A blast of cool air freshened the little room but did nothing to relieve the tension. Brother Daniel pressed his lips together and returned to his desk. He sat down and pulled a sheaf of essays toward him, squinting at them in the unsteady light. He picked up his pen, but put it down again and glowered at his niece. Her head was turned to the courtyard, her shoulders pulling toward it. Above the noise of the storm Frère Daniel heard laughter, voices giggling as several boys and girls, the latter dressed in *ao dais* and clutching their books above their heads to keep off the rain, raced into the classroom directly across from his cell. A tall blonde shadow darted in behind them and proceeded to the front. Kim Hong spun back to the desk.

"May I go, Uncle?" she said. "The class is starting."

A look of impatience flashed across Daniel's face.

"You've learned enough English," he said. "It's time these lessons should stop."

Kim Hong gasped in surprise, and Brother Daniel gazed down at his papers again. The words of Khai, his best student, seemed clichéd and stilted, and the pen hovered above the page, uncertain where first to strike. The room became hot and close once more, and the fragrance of Kim Hong's perfume failed before the musty smell of Daniel's books, the starchy odor of his collar, the sweat souring on his forehead. He glanced up. Kim Hong had turned pale, in spite of the rouge she'd applied to her cheeks and which he'd at first mistaken for her natural color.

"May I *go?*" she repeated.

He gripped the pen hard, irked by her insistence, and a jet of red ink spurted onto the page beneath him. He let out an exasperated cry, grabbed a cloth, and carefully dried Khai's essay. When he looked up again, Kim Hong was already halfway across the courtyard.

———

Brother Daniel saw that Khai had not arrived yet. He knelt down beside his rose plants, and with a small hand hoe he gently raked the rich dark loam, a finely ground mixture of peat and kitchen compost surrounding his Peace Rose, the first and most cherished of the lot. He examined the soil, running some of it critically through his fingers, then tugged on a seven-leafed sucker which had sprung up too near the base of the bush and extracted it expertly by the roots. It was early morning. The draft of cold air behind the brothers' residence worried him slightly, but the sweet aroma of the large-flowered Paul Shirville Heart Throb Rose, Khai's favorite, exploded in his face like a hothouse bloom. Frère Daniel set down his hoe, peered at the branches of the Peace Rose, and sighed. Even in the feeble light he could see that two tiny black spots had cropped up over-night on yet another leaf, which he now picked off between his thumb and forefinger. His mouth hardened with aggrava-tion as he peeked over the stone wall which screened Lasan Taberd off from Hai Ba Trung Street and the world. On top of a tall bamboo scaffold across the street several Vietnamese men worked away on the seventh floor of the new high rise, a maximum security American billet which towered above the school. Inside the half-built structure carpenters' hammers rang out; somewhere in the distance an electric saw buzzed; closer in a lathe whirred. Two white-suited workers carrying a girder angled in and out of the drywalled rooms of a large apartment, pith helmets on their heads to protect them from the sun. The smell of wood chips, mortar, and lime showered down on the cleric as the men dropped the heavy girder with a clunk and wiped their sweaty brows. Sun! When had he or his flowers last seen enough of *that?*

"I'm sorry I'm late, Brother," Khai said, hurrying up to him completely out of breath. The boy's *cravate* was awry, his collar was unbuttoned, and a crumb from his breakfast still stuck to his mouth. He glanced down at his Heart Throb and cried out in dismay. He took one of the salmon-pink flowers in his hand and plucked off an aphid that had crawled up from the branch, which was beginning to show unmistakable signs of fungus. "The lack of light is killing it, Brother," he complained, remov-ing several other insects. "What are we to do?"

Brother Daniel gazed at the construction across the street again and didn't answer. The day before, he'd looked up at the end of the hour from the papers he was grading to the classroom on the other side of the courtyard. His progress had been slow, his mind distracted by the memory of his unsatisfactory interview with Kim Hong. After the lesson ended, she remained behind and waited for Khai and the other students to leave, then walked out with the teacher. The tall American stood dangerously close to her, like the sucker which had threatened his Peace Rose. Kim Hong riveted her eyes on the man as he bent over her and whispered something, and she did not look even once at her uncle observing her sadly from his cell. . . .

"Brother?"

"I don't know, *mon fils*. I just don't know."

Frère Daniel reached up and snapped off another damaged leaf. On top of the new billet the hammers now rattled like a well-disciplined rifle battery. Brother Daniel watched as a yellow Caterpillar crane operated by an American grabbed a huge section of concrete wall and gingerly lifted it off the ground. The big foreign machine belched out a plume of black smoke and inched its way forward, and the cleric leaned over his Peace Rose to shield it from the noxious fumes. The crane driver maneuvered around the scaffolding and reached the building at last. The workers seized the section of wall and guided it into place, and Frère Daniel looked on grimly as the eighth floor began to take shape. He peered down at his Peace Rose again. Another square inch of the bush had faded into the shadows, like a planet on slow eclipse. He sighed a second time and gazed at Khai.

"When is that concert?"

The boy turned crimson and averted his eyes.

"Saturday, Brother." His voice barely rose above the din across the street.

Frère Daniel raked the ground thoughtfully with his hoe. After a minute he glanced up.

"Tell that teacher I want to see him in my room. Today, after class."

He scrambled to his feet and shook the dirt off his hands with a rapid swishing of the palms. Khai stared at him. "Are you *sure*, Brother?" he asked, his voice filled with alarm.

Frère Daniel looked at him sharply.

"Tell him."

———

They had come south together in September of 1954. When the Catholic refugees, Daniel, Kim Hong, her parents, and her younger brother Cac among them, fled Hanoi after the French left and the Viet Minh took over the North, the cleric and his niece became separated from the rest in Haiphong. Kim Hong was five, and Daniel had just graduated from the Christian Brothers seminary in Hanoi. His was the last class to do so. Kim Hong cried and cried and desperately clutched her uncle's hand as they watched her parents' freighter steam away without them. Shut in by a sudden typhoon which swirled in off of Hainan Island, they had to wait another two days to sail. When the moment arrived, Frère Daniel, in his clerical garb, hoisted the girl in his arms and approached the gangplank of a big American cargo ship under the watchful eyes of a couple of North Vietnamese soldiers, Ho Chi Minh's new conquerors. Dirty brown bilge water gushed from a pipe on one of the lower decks into the garbage-strewn harbor. The stench of decayed seaweed, of fuel oil from the already churning engines, of their unwashed fellow passengers as they all crowded nervously together at the foot of the gangway, rose in Frère Daniel's nostrils and made him wince. One of the Communist soldiers scowled at him, and Brother Daniel held his niece tight, as he might have clutched a sacred relic, and quickly carried her on board.

"Uncle," the child whispered, as soon as he set her down on the deck. "Who *are* they?" Her tiny wooden sandals clopped on the steel framework as she turned to him.

At first he thought she meant the soldiers, but then he saw several huge sailors on the quarterdeck in front of them. Their uniforms were immaculate, spotless, white as ivory, and their brightly polished shoes glittered in the morning light. They hurried about the deck helping the frightened, poorly clad Vietnamese with a self-assurance and efficiency that Brother Daniel found intimidating, and he felt mortified for his people as he noticed the contrast. A frail old woman laden down by her belongings slipped suddenly and cried out, and one of the sailors leaped forward, grabbed her by the elbow, and effortlessly relieved her of her burden. He flashed her a smile as bright as the sun, and Kim Hong clung to her uncle's cassock and gaped at the marvelous man in wide-eyed wonder. Frère Daniel set his mouth hard.

"They are Americans, child," he said. He took her by the hand and steered her toward an open hatchway off to their left. "They say they are here to help us, but I have my doubts. Why would anyone want to help *us?*"

Two of them were fast approaching, however, and Brother Daniel watched them apprehensively. But then he tripped on the hatch coaming, and he let go of Kim Hong's hand and clawed frantically at the railing. The girl screamed in terror, struck out with her foot, and plunged down into the darkness.

"Kim Hong!" Brother Daniel yelled, his voice gripped with horror. He seized the railing and stumbled down the stairs.

"It's okay, little one," a voice said. "I've got you."

Kim Hong sniveled in the arms of an American. Frère Daniel stared up into a face as strange and flat as the bewildering monotone the man had used with his niece, although the words themselves were familiar to him from long years of study at the seminary. The sailor towered above him, and Brother Daniel felt small and insignificant beside him. The American's aftershave gave off the cleanest scent he'd ever inhaled, and the cleric felt dirty as well. He was mortified again, this time for himself.

"I take her now," he said coldly, stretching his hand out toward his niece. Kim Hong clung to the American, and she dug her tiny fingers into his large muscular forearm. She gave her uncle a look of reproach, then buried her tear-stained cheek in the sailor's massive shoulder.

"It's okay, little one," the man said again. "You had quite a fall, eh?"

"You give her *now*," Frère Daniel ordered. He turned to his niece, but Kim Hong only burrowed deeper into the American's shoulder. The sailor laughed merrily.

"Ooh, don't cry now," he coaxed, letting her down gently on the deck. She struggled to climb back up into his arms, but the man stepped back and fished for something in his pocket. "Look!"

He brought out a small, colorful package which smelled of coconut and almonds. The child stopped sniffling and stared at the package with eager eyes. Brother Daniel shook his head, but Kim Hong reached her hand out. Tet, the only time for candy, was still four months away.

"No, thanks," the cleric said, interposing his hand between theirs. He scooped Kim Hong up and rudely turned his back on the American. Kim Hong kicked at him in protest as he bore her away. Brother Daniel's face burned with shame. *How dare the man bribe her like that!* He plodded along the corridor with no idea where he was going, ignoring the sailor's astonished exclamations behind him and the renewed wailings of his niece. . . .

———

"You wanted to see me?"

Brother Daniel glanced up from his grading and focused hard on the darkened doorway. The monsoon had turned the late afternoon into night. Rain clattered on the rooftop, and the battered aluminum lamp beside his writing table smoked dreadfully and gave off the pungent smell of kerosene. The electric generator powering the brothers' residence had broken down the minute the storm began. The American teacher stole into view and then stopped, as though unsure how to meet a holy man in his cell. Frère Daniel sensed his advantage and sprang to his feet.

"I will be *terre à terre, Monsieur,*" he said crisply. "It's about my niece."

The American remained where he was but shifted his rain-soaked books from one arm to the other. He looked to be about twenty-three and was even taller than Daniel had imagined. He'd been drenched by his sprint across the courtyard, but he held his head high and gazed placidly at the cleric in spite of the latter's abrupt announcement. Brother Daniel was dispirited by the man's height and quickly pointed to a simple wooden chair across from his desk.

"Please," he said, vexed that his hand shook. The man advanced into the room and sat down. He placed his books, *English for Today* and a workbook, on the corner of the desk. Brother Daniel sat down as well. The American's clothes smelled damp, but the rain had not been able to wash out his air of self-confidence or the powerful scent of his aftershave. Frère Daniel was more disconcerted than ever.

"Your niece?"

The cleric rose up in his chair and leveled his eyes at the visitor. Outside the wind picked up, and the rain pounded the pavement and swirled in rivulets into the gutters. The odor of sodden leaves drooping from the kapok tree filled Brother Daniel with sadness.

"She is so young, you see. Seventeen. Still a child, really. I'm sure you—"

"Who *is* your niece?"

Frère Daniel started and gazed suspiciously at his guest, trying to read his mind. His heart vacillated between hope and fear.

"Kim Hong. Tran Thi Kim Hong. She's in your class."

"Ah yes, Miss Hong," the man said with a smile. "The one who wears jeans."

A deep frown creased Brother Daniel's brow.

"Just so," he snapped. The American raised his eyebrows at the cleric's curtness, and Frère Daniel inclined his shoulders forward as though to apologize.

"She is quite . . . *susceptible*," he went on, more mildly. "Her parents died in a typhoon when we were coming south in 1954, and I had to place her in a sisters' residence in Da Kao. She couldn't live here with me, of course." He paused, but the American didn't say anything. "I'm afraid she gets very little guidance there, however." He shook his head and waited again, but the American still said nothing. "I do not want her to be led astray, *Monsieur*," he added, a trace of annoyance creeping back into his tone. "Kim Hong is a good girl, *vous savez*, but not very . . . worldly."

His lips parted in a thin smile, which froze at the American's unexpected response.

"She's a pretty girl, too. A *very* pretty girl."

The wind moaned against the casement, bringing with it the smell of the rain-swept courtyard. Brother Daniel felt a chill and rose from his desk. His voice suddenly became harsh.

"*Monsieur*, I cannot allow my niece to be subjected to corrupting influences, and I must therefore *insist* that you leave her alone. I have seen the way you take on with her. You cannot just come here and do whatever you please, you know."

The American shot to his feet, clearly offended. "I am her *teacher*," he said. "And you have no right to insult me. If you think that I don't—"

Frère Daniel cut him off.

"Please leave this room," he said. "Immediately." The American looked shocked, and the color drained from his face. Brother Daniel could not trust himself to point at the door, so he moved around the desk instead and ushered his visitor out. He lingered on the threshold until the man stomped through the gate onto Nguyen Du Street and strode away, his head unbowed by the driving rain. Then he turned and trudged back to his desk.

"Uncle, how *could* you?"

Brother Daniel fingered another dying bloom on his Peace Rose and did not glance up. He shifted uncomfortably, however, as Kim Hong, her voice choking, stepped forward and repeated her lament. Khai, who was standing nearby tending his Paul Shirville, flushed and looked away.

"How could you *talk* with him about me? It's disgraceful!"

The day was sweltering already, and storm clouds hovered on the horizon, ready to burst. The air was oppressive, and Frère Daniel's roses sagged forlornly and gave off the odor of faded perfume. The cleric longed for the end of the monsoon season; the incessant rains laden with pollution from the American war machine brought him and his flowers no comfort. But the end was still very far away. He gazed up at his niece at last.

"Speaking of disgraceful, look how you're dressed!" He plucked the leg of her jeans as though he was picking off another dead leaf from his Peace Rose. Kim Hong sprang back from him.

"He says you wrote him and demanded I transfer to old man Duc's class. Well, I . . . I won't do it!" Her voice choked up again, and tears welled in her eyes.

Brother Daniel's mouth twitched with anger.

"How dare you be so disrespectful!" he cried. He heard a rustling among the flowers and glared at Khai, who drew away from his Heart Throb and tried to make himself scarce among the other roses. "At least 'old man Duc' is a Vietnamese."

He was shaking all over now, and to calm himself he picked up his hoe and dug a hole around the base of his Peace Rose to give it more breathing room. The hoe struck an object, and he reached down into the hole and brought it up into the light. It looked like a rusted rifle bullet, but he couldn't be sure. In February 1859 the French had attacked the Saigon citadel. The eastern wall of Lasan Taberd was contiguous with one of the inner walls of the fortress. The citadel had fallen within hours, and Saigon had been under the thumb of one foreigner after another ever since. Brother Daniel stared at the object, disheartened, and then threw it angrily away. He turned back to his niece.

"I forbid you to go to this concert today," he said. "Instead you will return to the convent and discard those clothes, and on Monday you will go to Master Duc, properly dressed. Do you understand?"

Kim Hong looked stunned for a moment, and then she wheeled and stormed away without a word. Her sandals slapped the garden flagstones as she disappeared. Frère Daniel drew in a heavy breath and slowly released it. He bent forward and started to dig another hole around the base of his Peace Rose, but he soon gave it up and tossed down his hoe. Across the street a buzz saw whined. Khai puttered anxiously among the dying flowers.

———

As the afternoon drew to a close, Brother Daniel found it increasingly difficult to concentrate on the few remaining papers he had left to grade. The saws and hammers hemmed him in on both sides now, from the American billet at his back and the sound stage to his front. The CBC concert was to begin in fifteen minutes. In the middle of the courtyard, right under the kapok tree, a knot of workers hurried back and forth putting the finishing touches to the platform on which the band was to perform. At the front of the stage a simple red and yellow South Vietnamese flag fluttered alongside an American one, the stars of the latter covered over by a large white peace sign on a black background. The odor of eucalyptus wood, the grinding of the last board, and the shouts of the workers filtered past Daniel's door. On the far side of the platform the four band members, young Vietnamese with long stringy hair, bell-bottoms, and garishly colored tee shirts, warmed up on their electric guitars, piano, and drum set. The teeth-jarring wail of an American rock tune filled the courtyard. Brother Daniel scowled and massaged his sore forehead. He put his pen down and tramped out the door.

The last worker melted away, the irritating music stopped, and the wrought-iron gate of the school compound squealed back on its hinges. Hundreds of impatient teenagers dashed into the courtyard and streamed toward the stage. They were *all* dressed in jeans now, the boys in shirts, the girls in blouses. They swarmed around Frère Daniel but appeared hardly to notice him. The smell of their excited bodies rose above the sweet aroma of the kapok tree. Brother Daniel watched them scornfully as they milled about beneath the stage. How avidly they'd all succumbed to this filthy foreign trash! He thought of his *own* youth, and of the musicians in his village who had played traditional native folksongs on their *sao* flutes, tambours, and moon guitars. Songs of resistance, valor, love of country, fathers, and kings. He wheeled away in disgust and ran right into Khai.

"She's here, Brother," the boy said, in a pained voice. "Look!"

Frère Daniel turned and followed his gaze. He spotted the American first, overshadowing the crowd, edging his way forward. The cleric glowered at the man as he moved close to the stage, and then he shrank back in astonishment. At the American's side, blushing but firmly gripping his hand, was Kim Hong.

Brother Daniel stepped toward them just as the lead singer, a boy with a mustache and with his hair now tied in a ponytail to keep it away from his guitar, strode to the front of the stage.

"Thank for coming!" he yelled in English into a microphone. "We start with Beatle song! *She Love You!*"

The crowd applauded wildly, and the singer launched into the tune. The rest of the band took up the beat, and the crowd swayed back and forth to the music. Brother Daniel plunged in among them, batting away the swirling bodies and homing in on the American and his niece. Ecstatic voices everywhere sang along with the band, and the discordant, unfamiliar noises made the cleric's ears ache. For a moment he lost sight of them, and then he halted when they came into view again at the very foot of the stage. The American had his arms twined around Kim Hong and held her tight. The girl nuzzled against his chest. Her uncle looked on in anguish as she rose up on her toes and pressed her cheek affectionately into the man's shoulder. The American caressed her hair, and Kim Hong dropped back down on her feet and flashed him a joyful smile. Brother Daniel felt a spasm in his chest, as though his heart had lurched to a sudden stop.

He stared helplessly at the happy couple for a few seconds, while young people jostled and buffeted him on all sides, as if he was of no consequence. Then he turned on his heels and hobbled away toward his cell. Beneath the alcove of the brothers' residence, Khai loitered with a group of other young men. Red-faced with rage, the boy whispered rapidly to his comrades and pointed in the direction of the stage. One of the other Vietnamese youths nodded and bunched his fists. Frère Daniel marched up to them.

"Do not even *think* of it," he said sternly. "On the love of your Maker, you will do nothing. Do you hear me?"

The boy who had bunched his fists immediately relaxed them. "Yes, *mon frère,*" he murmured. Frère Daniel wheeled to Khai, who shuffled on his feet.

"Do *you* hear?"

Khai bit his lip, and a look of utter misery crossed his face. "Yes, Brother," he muttered. He quickly stalked away, and the others followed after him.

Brother Daniel gazed disconsolately at his cell. The CBC had started a set of songs by someone the lead singer called "Jefferson Airplane," and the horrific sounds were enough to drive him mad. He knew he could do no grading now, and so he crept to the end of the long building to find refuge among his flowers. The loud noises persecuted him even here, but he feasted his eyes on his Peace Rose and sought solace from its few remaining blooms. He glanced at the Heart Throb next to it and started. The head had been snapped clean off. Frère Daniel was overcome with sorrow. The dead plant reminded him of all the Vietnamese revolutionaries decapitated by the French for resisting their conquest. . . . Another yowling line of hideous American music burst upon his ears, and he looked back at the Peace Rose and tenderly fingered a fading blossom that was just beginning to turn brown. A swatch of tarpaulin protecting the building across the street snapped in the wind, and he lifted his head and glared at the big American billet. The workers had been busy all day and had made great progress on the eighth floor. When the morning returned, Brother Daniel knew he would find a little less sun left to cheer his Peace Rose, and he bowed his head in dejection. Gradually, of course, the foreigners would take even *that* away from him, and then what would he do? A wave of panic swept over him as he saw himself tumbling headlong into a terrifying black hole, but with no one at the bottom to catch him. He shuddered violently, and then, when the fear subsided, he leaned forward, pressed his thumb against his forefinger, and plucked the blossom off the dying rose.

nine

ENVY

In the back of the bus bouncing along the Ho Chi Minh trail, Diep fiddled with her cosmetic kit. The mother-of-pearl clasp shot open to reveal vermillion, white, and black, in the dim glow cast by the light above her head. The faint scent of makeup drifted upward and enclosed her in its smell. The actress gazed upon the colors of a warrior, Trieu Au, one of Viet Nam's most famous female generals, whom she was to play that night. She looked at the colors hopefully, but then her eyes glazed over. Heroines are not made from paint, she reminded herself. *Snap,* and the clasp closed.

The bus swerved to avoid a bomb crater, and Diep knocked against the window and then, recovering, stared out at the shells of the *lim* and pine trees recently blasted into nothingness by the big American bombers. Dew dripped off the pane and bathed her cheek, and Diep recoiled from its chill. The trees crept eerily toward her in the half-light of the foggy night, like wandering souls begging to be let in, and when the wind howled through the dead branches like paid mourners at a funeral, the girl shivered. She thought with relief and remorse of another battle she had missed.

Like Trieu Au, Diep had grown up with the idea that her highest duty was to answer her country's endless calls to war. But unlike the brave general she had simply looked on while her brothers—all except the youngest, Tran—and even her sisters had marched into the mangrove swamp behind their village and melted into Vietnamese history. How illustrious it was to be a war hero! the girl thought. She flicked open the makeup kit again. But also how dangerous.

The odor of cosmetics was less distinct now, as though the heroism had died out of Trieu Au's war paint. The bus veered around another bomb crater, and Diep's foot scraped against the golden shield she would don that evening. In 248 A.D., Trieu Au fled to the mountains after killing her wicked sister-in-law and raised one thousand troops to fight the Chinese. Diep thought of her *own* sister-in-law, or rather *ex*-sister-in-law, Giang, and scratched angrily at a gash in the vinyl seat back in front of her. Then she grabbed a mirror and held it up to the light. She gazed at herself, and the lines around her mouth slowly relaxed. Her face was still the most exquisite thing she'd ever seen, notwithstanding the snide remarks of the conceited city girl who'd married Tran.

"Hey, Diep!" a man called, on the other side of the aisle. Bac folded the newspaper he was reading and wheeled to stare at her for the fifth time that hour. "Nguyen Thi Vang's going to be there, isn't she?"

Snap.

Diep grimaced. The stench of diesel fuel drifted through the floorboards, but it was not that which made her nauseous. Bac repeated his question, and Diep kept her lips sealed and stared out the window again. But then she turned hot with annoyance and glared at him.

"I suppose so," she said gruffly. "What of it?"

She fiddled with the lid of the cosmetic case again, which was encrusted with cheap jewels that were the envy of the other girls in the acting troupe. Yet Manager Hung's gift didn't give her any enjoyment.

Bac unfolded his newspaper and tapped it excitedly.

"She's just been promoted to Song Thanh Field Commander, that's what!" he exclaimed. He stared at her still, and Diep returned his look coldly.

Who was this puny girl anyway? Diep had seen the famous photograph, published the year before, of President Ho Chi Minh pinning the Order of Liberation Medal to Nguyen Thi Vang's chest. Vang stood at attention, with the flattened nose, protruding jaw, and vacant stare of a macaque. She appeared frightened and pathetic, and if she hadn't had the supposed luck to shoot down six American airplanes all by herself, no one would ever have noticed her. Yet now she was a heroine!

"Hey, they've run the picture of her receiving the medal from Uncle Ho again! Wanna see? She's quite fetching!"

Diep angrily shook her head. What fools men were! She flopped forlornly in her seat and swallowed her pride. And to think she had to put on her best performance for the little nobody in a few hours!

———

"Why are you doing this?" Tran wailed.

It was the summer of 1966, and Diep had been living in Hanoi for two years. She'd busied herself helping Pho, the maid, scrub vegetables in the kitchen. Jicama, green onions, bitter melon, pigeon peas, even a Dalat asparagus which she'd managed to smuggle in past Giang's ferret eyes. Her sister-in-law made them scrounge after every piaster while she hoarded up as much as she could to advance her "career." Battles broke out over almost every expenditure, and Diep, at nineteen, felt like the orphaned Trieu Au, forced to live like a slave in her brother's household.

"Answer me!"

The baby started to cry at the agony in Tran's voice, sharp as the cleaver with which Pho hacked off the heads of the milkfish she tossed into the stewpot on the stove. The smell of kerosene, a city product, clung to the late afternoon air like a woolen cloak and made Diep feel light-headed. It had rained an hour earlier, but it was miserably hot again.

"How can you just go like this?"

Pho darted past Diep and grabbed the infant off the floor. "Come, baby. Let's go out onto the porch."

The screen door scraped as Pho pulled it shut behind her, and Diep's niece's sobbing grew faint.

"Giang?"

Diep laid aside her scrub brush, wiped her hands on the terry cloth towel she'd tucked into her pantaloons, and stepped into the parlor. She glanced worriedly at her brother, who'd collapsed on the divan next to the window. The smell of oranges and star fruit gone bad on the family altar drifted across the room. Tran pounded his fist into the sofa cushion. The sound was muffled, sad, like the futile beating of a corpse. Plumes of dust rose from the pillow like ashes.

Giang lolled in the doorway. Diep studied her lipstick, her nails, the sequins on the silk *ao dai* she'd worn to the interview, the porcelain barrette, the stiletto heels. They were all red, the color of luck, reflections of Giang's unbounded confidence when she'd left the house that morning.

"They're paying my way to France for three years to study cinema. And I'm going."

Diep's heart leaped. A film star! In Europe! What wouldn't *she* give for such an opportunity! Her eyes widened in envy, but then narrowed guiltily when she saw the stricken look on her brother's face. Giang stared at him blankly. Diep felt resentment rise inside her like a poisonous vapor. Indeed, how *could* she do this to them?

"Coward!" she yelled. "You're just fleeing the country because you're afraid of the war!"

Giang flinched, then stepped away from the door.

"Why, you drab little mouse!" she said scornfully. "Just look at you!" In her high heels Giang looked a lot taller than she was, like a screen goddess already, and as she got closer Diep shrank back unwillingly. She glanced at Tran, who impotently beat the cushion still. Giang followed her gaze, a sneer of contempt fixed to her mouth. As she looked at her, Diep understood how Trieu Au had found it so easy to kill the cruel and cantankerous witch who'd oppressed her until she was twenty. Suddenly she erupted.

"What kind of wife and mother *are* you? Who ever heard of a Vietnamese woman deserting her family? You *must* be a coward."

Giang wheeled on her. Her eyes gleamed malevolently. She raised her hand as if to strike, but held it back as though she was afraid of injuring her nails.

"You should feel honored," she said calmly. "As should your brother. Only the *beautiful* ones get to go to Paris."

She paused. Diep's shoulders trembled with wrath. Giang flashed her perfect white teeth at her.

"The others must stay behind."

———

The outdoor dressing room lay in a grove of nutmeg and clove trees next to a clearing where several cadres were busy constructing a crude plywood stage. The monsoon had ended just before they arrived. The day was warm still, and the heavy, moisture-laden Lao wind which snaked out of the mountains stroked Diep's cheek as she pranced at the head of the acting troupe like Trieu Au followed by her train. Ngoc, the turnip-faced troll who played the role of her bargewoman, muttered something uncomplimentary behind her, but Diep stuck her nose in the air and focused on a lovely stand of crape myrtle straight ahead, set off by aromatic clumps of buttercups and gentians. The dressing tables stood in the middle of the colorful plant life, and Diep's heart gladdened as though the artillery unit had deliberately gathered all this beauty in her honor. In the distance, reflected in the late afternoon sunlight, the Song Thanh River twined like a silver bracelet around the wrist of a banyan-studded island. The smell of flowers and wet spices reminded her of a richly scented tea, something reserved for royalty alone. Diep felt exhilarated and held her head even higher.

Another squad of cadres dug up the cogon grass around the stage for an air-raid trench. Several soldiers stopped working and turned their heads appreciatively as Diep sauntered by.

"Hi," she simpered at a tall, shy-looking young man half-hidden behind a kauri tree. She put him out of countenance by giving him a sunbeam smile and flapping her eyelashes.

"Hi," the man gulped. He immediately averted his eyes. Diep swept proudly on, a conqueror in her own domain every bit as successful as Trieu Au had been in hers. What a shame it would be to mar a face like hers with the ugly realities of war! She sat down at one of the tables and thought of Giang. Her sister-in-law had divorced Tran in France and was still skulking around Paris among the other vermin of the sewers, she supposed, while *she* held court in the jungle. . . . The actress smiled exultantly.

"Who does she think she *is?*" Ngoc said. Diep tensed and turned her head. The bargewoman sat with the others at an adjoining table. Diep glowered at the whole group, then showed them her back and opened her wooden dressing box. "Just because old man Hung—"

"Just because old man Hung *what?*"

Ngoc jumped in her seat. The manager stood above her, his arms folded. His greasy hair was swept back from his brow in a sporty fashion, but his jowls quivered pudgily and his teeth snapped at Ngoc in two disjointed yellow rows, like parched corn rotting on the stalk.

"Nothing, boss," Ngoc mumbled. She ducked her head and nervously fingered the burlap jerkin she was to wear that night. Diep slid her palms along the silky smooth surface of Trieu Au's magenta blouse and gloried in the contrast. The warrior's golden helmet dazzled her with its brilliance, and she held it up for all to see. Ngoc gave it an irritated glance, and Diep's face glowed with triumph.

The glittering helmet must have caught Hung's eyes, too, for he wheeled, grinned at Diep, and skipped to her side. He spotted her cosmetic case.

"So, Miss Princess, when are you going to show me how much you appreciate my little present? It's been five months, you know."

A thin stream of spittle drooled from his mouth and lodged in his scraggly beard, and Diep felt overcome by revulsion. She twisted away from him and reached for her eyeliner.

"Well, how about it?" he said, leaning over her. Out of the corner of one eye, the beautiful lash of which she extended with a brush, Diep saw him place his arms akimbo and strike a jaunty pose. But his smell reminded her of the drunken water carrier who used to pick through the garbage in their Hanoi neighborhood, and she screwed up her mouth in disdain.

"Please," she said. "Can't you see I'm busy?"

Just then Bac ran up to them, his face glowing with excitement.

"Manager Hung! Guess what? She's done it again!"

The manager spun to his subordinate and contracted his brow. Diep worked on her other eyelash, which was just as lovely as the first.

"Who?" Hung said.

"Why, Nguyen Thi Vang, of course!" Bac tugged the boss's sleeve. "Yesterday she shot down another American airplane, and a foreign film crew is coming to do a documentary on her! They're expected any minute."

"Really!"

The manager's jaw waggled in wonder. Diep's mascara stick twitched in her hand, and she glanced in the mirror and frowned. She snatched a tissue and furiously rubbed the makeup off, but she had to steady her hand before she could apply it again.

"Well, let's go then!"

Quick as a mouse deer hopping through a meadow Manager Hung was gone from her side, but instead of feeling relieved, Diep sagged like a waterside hut collapsing on its pilings. Would the luck of this pathetic nonentity never end? She darted an irate look at Hung's departing back, but then her hand froze as she lifted the mascara stick again. She gazed into the mirror, stupefied. Her face had contorted itself into the repulsive mug of Nguyen Thi Vang, and in the background she saw the ghostly image of Giang fleering at her as well. Diep wheeled around, but except for a thin wreath of mist swirling among the clove trees there was nothing to be seen. Not even the wood spirits that haunted the forest. When she looked in the mirror again, her own beautiful face beamed reassuringly back at her. But she was enraged at the evil trick Vang and Giang had just played on her.

"Who do they think they are?" she cried, little realizing she was echoing Ngoc's words. Diep's eyes glistened darkly, and the lovely lashes now fluttered with the desire for revenge. But there was no one at the adjoining table to notice. They'd all gone off to pay homage to the heroine of Song Thanh.

———

Nguyen Thi Vang perched on the turret of the new SU 23mm cannon which Moscow had donated to the cause of Vietnamese liberation and awaited the arrival of the European film crew. Diep crept in among the large crowd gathered to watch the show. A breeze shivered the branches of the melaleuca above her, and her feet sank, like fingers into dough, into the rich black loam surrounding the tree trunk. She looked down and wiggled her sandals free, but as she did so she knocked loose a scent as ancient as the forest itself, before the time of warriors, actresses, and envy. For a moment she thought of her humble village upbringing and wavered in her purpose. But then a gurgle of dismay came from the turret, and she glanced up. As she did so, intense satisfaction crept over her. Nguyen Thi Vang was even homelier than she'd imagined.

The great war heroine cringed beside the gun barrel and held on to it for dear life. Diep slipped from behind the melaleuca, the taste of victory sweet on her tongue, and positioned herself directly opposite her. *What a quailing atom she is!* the actress thought. Vang's face squinched like a mole's when she spotted her, and her cheek muscles quivered uncontrollably. Diep felt heavenly. Heroine indeed! At least Trieu Au had *looked* like one.

"Where's that film crew?" Vang asked, addressing no one in particular. "I want to get this over with!"

She rocked anxiously on the gun deck and cast her eyes about. Her gaze stopped at someone behind Diep.

"Quy!" she cried, then blushed and shrank behind the gun. Diep twisted round, bubbling with curiosity, and as she did so someone pitched forward as though to help the distressed war heroine. Instead he stepped on the actress's foot. Diep winced.

"Oh, I'm sorry," he said. "I didn't mean—"

The man's voice suddenly ended in a gasp. Diep recognized the shy young cadre she'd entranced earlier. His glance fell to the ground, but then he popped his head back up and peered timidly at her.

"Why, *hello* there," Diep said, in her most melodious voice. Her mind mulled over the look Vang had just flashed him. Quy glanced away again, but soon gave up the struggle.

"It's okay, you don't have to apologize," Diep said. "It didn't hurt a bit."

The man looked relieved, but then several big drops of perspiration broke out on his forehead. The sweat rather flattered her, since it was a very cool day, and Diep rewarded him with a smile.

"It's okay," she repeated, salting her voice with just the right trace of emotion. She emitted an awkward little cough and turned back to the artillery piece as though she, too, was embarrassed. Nguyen Thi Vang emerged from behind the gun and glared at them, and Diep's skin prickled with joy. But then Manager Hung sprang onto the gun turret and gallantly extended his hand.

"Come, Miss Vang!" he exclaimed. "Don't be afraid! I'll help you!"

With a grand strut he led the veteran forward as though to the front of a stage. His eyes swept the crowd. Diep gave him a dirty look. To think that only a few minutes earlier the ungrateful fool had tried to cash in on his present to her!

"You see, Miss Vang," he said, flapping his hand about, "we are all your friends." Nguyen Thi Vang clung to his arm. "*I am your friend.*"

His eyes met Diep's, and he turned back quickly to the woman at his side. Vang clung to him even more tightly.

"Fear not," he said. "I shall see you safely through the interview. Bring them on!"

He smirked and patted her hand, and Diep's tongue went gravelly with the ashes of disgust. Hung peered back at her, and Diep kept the sneer on her face until his brow darkened and he looked away again. He crooked his finger at Bac, who climbed up onto the gun deck beside him. Hung leaned over and whispered in his ear, while Nguyen Thi Vang's glance raked the crowd. After a few seconds Bac nodded and jumped off the turret. Diep spotted Quy goggling at her from a respectful distance now. She made a face at him, and he was instantly at her side. A cry of apprehension burst from Nguyen Thi Vang's throat, and the actress thrilled as though it was the loveliest sound she'd heard in years. But then Bac sidled up to her and tapped her on the elbow.

"Psst! Diep!"

"What?" she said brusquely. She turned, and the look in his eye filled her with foreboding.

"Manager Hung wants you to forget about Trieu Au."

Diep stared at him, speechless. Bac pursed his lips.

"He wants you to play Miss Vang instead."

———

Diep stamped about the makeshift stage. Her eyes glowered at every object they lit upon, and she clawed at the cheap cotton uniform Manager Hung had ordered her to wear for her portrayal of Nguyen Thi Vang as though the coarse fabric was an insult to her body. Trieu Au's golden armor lay discarded on a side table, where it gleamed dully in the light of a single oil lantern. Only when she donned one of Vang's floppy field caps and launched into her first speech would they risk another lantern or two. The French film crew had not yet arrived, and there were rumors of renewed American bombing up the Ho Chi Minh trail which accounted for the delay. Diep's glance darted to the empty benches before her, and at the wicker chair planted like a throne in the middle of the first row. Her eyes burned through it like the sun through a magnifying glass.

A gong clanged, and the audience began to ramble in. Diep's chest heaved as Trieu Au's must have on the memorable day the Chinese surrounded her and she tried to flee in a basket boat. Now *she*, too, knew what it felt like to have the oppressors close in on her. Vang waltzed in on Hung's arm and sat in the place of honor beside him. Diep glared at her. The two of them were dressed exactly alike now, and an ill-natured person might have said they were twins. Nguyen Thi Vang smiled triumphantly at her. Black and scarlet hatred smoldered in the actress's breast.

The gong sounded a second time. Manager Hung pressed Vang's hand and nodded at the stage. Diep rammed the heroine's cap down on her head and slogged forward.

In the days of the evil invader . . . a common girl, a mere slip of a thing . . . unremarkable as a paddy crab . . .

Diep lisped the scandalous words joyfully, her eyes fixed on Vang's. The heroine's face became pallid for a second, then returned to its natural muddy hue. Several people in the audience shifted uncomfortably, however.

. . . doubting her courage . . . with good reason . . .

Annoyed looks now, some murmuring even, and Diep leaned over to pick up a machine gun, the only prop on stage. She could easily handle the 12.7mm by herself, but she stumbled expertly on the foot Quy had stepped on as she strained to lift it. She cried out and looked round helplessly at the audience. Then she fumbled a well-rehearsed line and gulped as if she was on the verge of panic. She stared at the audience again, importunately this time. Quy was beside her in a flash. Diep caught a whiff of his cologne and was elated to think he'd spruced himself up just for her.

"Let me help you!" he blurted out, then flushed at the realization he was not supposed to speak. Diep melted him with her most tender glance. The muttering in the audience picked up as they lifted the machine gun together, but Diep ignored it. She let her hands rest on Quy's as they propped the gun up and pointed it into the sky. She made sure the way she squeezed his fingers was visible to all.

> *This commoner, I say, struggling to hide the awful truth which lay hidden in her heart . . .*

A yelp of astonishment came from the front row. Diep gently stroked Quy's knuckles and gave him another sweet look, while out of the corner of her eye she watched Vang fume. The actress rubbed up against him as though to help steady the machine gun, and Quy turned red. His hands pulsated, and his knees began to buckle. Diep suddenly released her hold and stepped away, and the machine gun teetered in his hands and then crashed to the ground. Diep wheeled to the audience and covered her face in pretended shame.

> *At the moment of trial she was unable to go on. . . . What luck, then, brought down the enemy in spite of her cowardly soul?*

A howl of outrage rent the night air, and Diep got no further. Through the screen of her fingers she saw Nguyen Thi Vang bounce furiously to her feet. Figures raced about, and for a moment she thought they were going to rush her. But there was a strange excitement in their voices, and Diep widened her fingers and noticed that the audience had all gathered around someone new. She took her hands away from her face and caught her breath.

"What are *you* doing here?"

Giang had managed to remain ravishing in spite of the ordeal she and the French film crew had gone through. Her shirt was indeed torn, and there was a hole in the trousers around one knee, but the cut on her lip only made her mouth look fuller and rosier than ever, and notwithstanding the straw and dust, her hair still shimmered with a healthy sheen that could only have been the product of an expensive European shampoo. The scent of her perfume and the look which flickered from her bewitching black eyes mesmerized the audience, and they all stood frozen, like helpless insects trapped in the sap of a Timor gum tree. Giang's two cameramen stood to one side.

"We're here to film Nguyen Thi Vang, of course," she said, fixing her eyes on her ex-sister-in-law. "What are *you* doing here?" Without waiting for an answer, she turned up her nose and looked away. Diep colored up with real shame this time.

"We had some trouble with an American bomber near Ban Tasseng," Giang explained, addressing the entire crowd now. "But I got some good footage to take back to *Paris*."

Oohs and aahs at the magic place name. The crowd closed in admiringly around her. More exclamations of awe, each one cutting Diep like a knife. Tears of frustration pooled in her eyes.

"Where *is* Miss Vang, by the way?" Giang asked. She looked about her. The heroine of Song Thanh stepped bashfully forward, her head lowered as if before a queen. With a smile of indulgence, Giang raised the trembling girl's chin.

"Don't be shy, *Sister*," she said, casting a pointed glance at Diep. The actress's brow blackened at the word. "Remember, you're a Heroine of the State!"

As if on cue a siren sounded, and something dark streaked out of the sky toward them. There was a loud explosion, then another. Nguyen Thi Vang dashed to the machine gun which

Quy had dropped, picked it up, and opened on the American airplane. Giang whisked to her side, microphone in hand. The film crew sprang into action and aimed its camera at her.

Diep stepped forward as though to join them, then shivered and remained where she was. The rest of the crowd scattered to various positions to fight the enemy. Explosions sounded all around them now. Someone barged into the actress and ran on.

"Quy!" she called, in her silkiest voice. She composed herself to award him her most winning smile, but he didn't even turn. Instead he flew to Vang's elbow and knelt beside her. He held the cartridge belt for her, feeding bullet after bullet into the machine gun. Vang gave him a brief but grateful look. Giang stood shoulder to shoulder with her, speaking calmly into the microphone.

Diep could barely contain her dismay as she watched the three of them. After a few moments she wheeled and stumped away in the direction of the forest. Her shoulders sloped toward the ground. Trapped by the Chinese, Trieu Au was forced to admit defeat at last, and the actress thought of how the great general had drowned herself to escape capture, dying with her honor intact and her reputation secure. At the edge of the trees Diep stopped and glanced up at the sky, and for the space of a heartbeat she longed to encounter a kindly bomb which had managed to elude her enemies' perfect quest for greatness. Then she bowed her head and trudged into the forest.

ten

THE COMPOSER
AND THE MERMAID

He had not realized how difficult it was to complete another man's work. Camille Saint-Saëns had had a rough passage out to Poulo Condor on the Messageries Maritimes mail packet from Cap St. Jacques. It was March 1895, and an unusual early spring storm roiled the South China Sea into mountainous waves of emerald green foam which crested on all sides of the ship. Camille hung his head over the railing and vomited several times. The governor of the archipelago, M. Descelles, clearly honored to have France's greatest living composer on board, stayed by his side solicitously the whole time and tried to comfort him by telling him how Marco Polo himself had taken refuge on Poulo Condor from a storm on his way home from China in 1294. The adventures of the famous explorer did little to quell the heaving of Camille's stomach, but the voyage was nothing compared to his struggle to finish Ernest Guiraud's opera.

On the third day the wind and rain which had lashed the chain of islands since his arrival finally lifted from the sea, like a curtain rising on a new act, and Camille joyously stepped out onto the portico of the guest house with a steaming tisane in his hand. He settled himself contentedly into the sturdy rattan rocker which his servant Tam had taken from a protected nook outside the maitre's bedroom window that morning and dragged into the sunlight. Camille was resolved to tackle the great work at last. He took a tentative sip from his tisane, which burst with the fragrance of a thousand herbs and flowers, reminding him of his friend Monet's famous garden at Giverny, and gazed at the ocean rippling blue and placidly now, a pulse at rest. Sailors armed with soap and water scrubbed the concrete dock at which he'd landed until it was as white as chalk. The smell of bleach carried to the porch. The slate gray blockhouse of a prison rose forbiddingly above a jagged bauxite cliff off to his right, but it did not dampen his spirits. It was such a magnificent day! The sun sparkled on the waves like spangles on the dress of a beautiful woman, and the gentle breeze, warmed and sweetened by the evergreens at his back and the clove and almond trees on the rockbound shore in front of him, filled Camille with gladness. His fingers caressed the arm of the rocker, smooth and white as the tusks of an old dugong, one of the funny sea cows resting like mermaids on the rocks in the harbor and gazing dreamily out to sea. Just like that the first few bars of the third act came to him.

"Hey, Tam! Quick!" Success had fattened Camille, and at the age of sixty he was finding it hard to clamber to his feet. "My score!"

The servant ran up to him almost immediately. Without a word he held out the exquisite ivory fountain pen which Beauvais, the director of the Theatre Lyrique, had given the renowned composer in honor of the grand opening of *Le Timbre d'argent* eighteen years earlier, along with the great wad of papers which Guiraud had bequeathed him on his deathbed. The first two acts of *Brunhilda*. Saint-Saëns snatched the sheaf from the servant's hand, found a blank page, and set to work, balancing the heavy score on the arm of the rocker. Tam stood by and respectfully looked on.

"*Mais bien sur, bien sur!*" Camille exclaimed, as the pen flew across the page. Ideas galloped madly in his head, and he could barely contain his excitement long enough to write the notes down. But then a horn blasted in the harbor, and the composer glanced up in irritation.

A steam launch approached the quay, its funnel belching smoke into the clear blue sky. A number of local fishing craft darted in and out around it. The launch reminded Saint-Saëns of the boat from Lucerne to Tribschen twenty-five years earlier, in July 1870. The title of Guiraud's opera had stirred up the unpleasant memory. Camille peered balefully at the boat as it docked.

"Tam! *Qu'est-ce que c'est?*"

The servant stepped forward and glanced at the quay.

"The prison ship, maître," he whispered reluctantly. A group of Vietnamese men and women, dressed in gray and linked by chains, emerged from the bowels of the launch and tottered toward the gangplank under the watchful gaze of a squadron of soldiers.

The composer's eyes drifted back to the blockhouse, but then the next few measures came to him, and his pen raced across the page again. Suddenly he stopped and rubbed his hands together. Now he knew why he'd found the job so trying. *Brunhilda* indeed! Even though Wagner's operas were the last thing on Guiraud's mind when he named the piece after an obscure sixth-century queen of France, the title still oppressed Camille, and he vowed to change it the minute he finished his task. His eyes flickered with fire as he resumed work, and the long line of captives being kicked and dragged up the steep slope in front of him barely registered on his brain. Hadn't he lived under *that* man's shadow for too long already?

———

The Composer and the Mermaid　　139

While he waited for the boat to Tribschen, Camille idled away the time by studying the double-sided roof panels on the Kapellbrucke, the ancient wooden bridge angled around the Wasserturm in the middle of the River Reuss. He strolled leisurely from panel to panel, his engagement present for Richard and Cosima, a fastidiously wrapped mahogany Chinois memento case, tucked under one arm. It had rained for several days before his arrival, and the planks of the bridge were still dank. The smell of mold was everywhere. Panel Number 1, the first Lucerner, a giant, reminded him of Fafner and Fasolt, and a twinge of envy hit him. *Das Rheingold* had premiered the previous September and was the rage of all Europe, casting its shadow into every corner and leaving little daylight for Camille or anyone else. . . . He slid his tongue from side to side in annoyance and moved quickly on, past Number 3, the Hofkirche; Number 6, Lucerne around 1600; Number 15, St. Beatus; and Number 26, Winkelried slaying the dragon. The dragon again reminded him of the fabulous legend which Wagner had set so successfully to music, and he gave the picture a cursory glance filled with spite. But then up ahead, at Panel 31, a dirty, unkempt crowd stared idiotically at Wilhelm Tell shooting the apple off his son's head, and Camille's envy gave way to pride. He peered haughtily at the rabble and took a long consolatory pinch of snuff. Wasn't he here at Richard's express invitation, *he,* Saint-Saëns, one of the chosen among the gods? Just like Liszt, Cosima's father, Friedrich Nietzsche, even King Ludwig of Bavaria. Camille swaggered off the bridge and blinked in the brilliant sunshine. A breeze from the river brought him the scent of irises and delphiniums, some Alpenfloren he couldn't identify, and his spirits gradually brightened. The journey would be worth it after all! But as the launch pulled away from the wharf and the sun pierced the crystalline lake like the rays which stabbed the River Rhine and lit up the Rheingold for Alberich's greedy searching eyes, Camille bristled with envy again. . . .

———

The next night was a stormy one. March was the best month to visit the archipelago, Governor Descelles had told him, promising the great composer a tranquil stay, but the deities who ruled the winds and the waves had apparently decided otherwise. The former howled about the eaves all evening, while the ocean roared in Camille's ears with a crescendo to which he was, of course, abnormally sensitive. The smell of salt and sea hung in the air around him. The shutters slammed against the wall outside his window with a persistent bang, and the composer tossed and turned on his bed trying to pick out the meter. The noise reminded him of the German bombardment of Paris in January 1871, during which he'd attempted to distract his petrified mind by registering the pitch of each shell as it whistled overhead. . . . Then came the rains, pattering on the tin roof of the guesthouse like a field drum. Camille rose from the bed cranky and out of sorts. Even Tam's tisane failed to mollify him.

"Get up, *mon cher!*" a voice called from the portico, shortly after ten. "The storm has passed!"

Governor Descelles poked his head through the door. His dapper white uniform and ridiculous-looking Panama hat provoked the composer even more than the wretched weather. There was also a vacuous grin on the man's face, and Camille was tempted to smack it off with the back of his hand. "*Quelle nuit, hein?* Shall we go for a walk?"

Saint-Saëns passed his fingers through his disheveled hair and grumbled a noncommittal response. But he shuffled to his feet, well aware he would accomplish nothing of consequence that day. He was still irked with Guiraud for starting Act Two of *Brunhilda* with simple figurations of E flat, just like Wagner at the beginning of the Ring cycle. Had the man ever realized what a puppet he was? But Camille also had reservations about the staccato phrasing he himself had written into some of the violin parts in the third act, knowing how weak and unreliable the strings at the Opera Comique were. Inevitably he'd have to change the parts to legati. What mediocrity he had to put up with!

"All right," he groused, snatching up a cigarette and thrusting it between his lips. "Just let me change."

But he was exhausted before he'd taken five steps off the portico, and he regretted his decision to come along. Descelles mentioned how delighted he was with Camille's visit and hinted broadly at how nice it would be if his noted guest would put in a good word for him back in Saigon, so he could get himself promoted off the island by the end of the year. Saint-Saëns trod disconsolately beside him. Why couldn't the meddlesome fellow leave him alone? The breeze had turned sour overnight, and the smell of decayed seaweed and rotting fish supplanted the sweet odors of the day before. A rook cawed gloomily in one of the almond trees as they passed. Camille was downcast. Halfway along the strand Descelles suddenly wheeled, and the composer almost ran into him.

"Would you like to go see our freshwater lake?" The governor's voice quavered, and his nervousness filled Camille with misgiving. "Quang Trung, it's called. It's up in the mountains, surrounded by a lush mangrove forest. The view is quite mag—"

"No!" Camille barked. He'd just spotted a group of persons clustered at the shore's edge, and he pointed to them. "I want to go *there*."

The bureaucrat followed the composer's gaze. His face turned the color of his uniform.

"There? Why, I don't think that's a good idea. You see. . . ."

He tried to block Camille's view, but the composer slipped around him, his fatigue quite gone now. About fifteen Vietnamese, male and female, hunkered down on a breakwater surrounded by sea grass. Several well-armed soldiers stood guard over them. The prisoners clawed at the coral at their feet, using their bare hands to extract the huge chunks and then setting them aside on the sand. Saint-Saëns stepped out onto the breakwater and was met by a scowl from one of the gendarmes. The composer ignored him and peered at the prisoner closest to him. The razor-edged coral had cut the girl's hands, both of which were raw and bleeding. The sight disturbed him greatly. At that moment Governor Descelles climbed up onto the rocks, and Camille turned to him.

"What are these people doing?" he asked angrily. His arm cast a wide net over the prisoners, like a conductor ranging over his orchestra. He stared at his companion, but Descelles merely licked his lips.

"*Well?*" Camille persisted.

"Really, *mon cher*, you should not be here," the governor said. "They are revolutionaries who must work off their crimes against the state. The coral they are gathering will be turned into lime." He turned and indicated a building off to the side of the prison. "In the factory."

The girl's hands continued to haunt Camille. "Who is that woman?" he said. "What has she done?"

Descelles peeked briefly at the girl.

"I don't know. One of the prisoners, of course. She probably just arrived."

Saint-Saëns thought of the steam launch from the day before, the one which had reminded him of his journey across Lake Lucerne so long ago. Within months of that memorable trip thousands of his fellow countrymen and women had become prisoners of the Germans, and their lot had been miserable indeed. Camille's eyes fell on the girl again, and compassion flowed through him. Her blood-soaked fingers moved him almost to tears. He spun round to the governor.

"I want her released."

Descelles started.

"Released? Why, that's impossible, maitre. Surely you know that."

Saint-Saëns bridled. "I know nothing of the kind, but I *can* see that this poor woman is suffering. Look at her hands!"

Descelles glanced at the girl again, then turned a look of stupid indifference on his guest. Camille struggled hard against his mounting indignation.

"*Que voulez-vous?*" he said. "Where could she possibly go? It's 90 kilometers to the mainland! I *want* her released."

The Composer and the Mermaid   143

Governor Descelles's mouth moved as though he was about to object, but the composer cut him off.

"Or shall I inform the Governor-General of your obduracy when I return to Saigon?"

M. Descelles's face went slack with fear. He sought the eye of the gendarme who hovered over the prisoner.

"Let her go."

———

A chill wind swept in from the Glarus Alps, notwithstanding the early summer weather, and swirled across Lake Lucerne. Camille shivered and sheltered himself in the lee of the pilot house until the boat landed at Tribschen. But once he stepped off onto the lawn and was in Richard's embrace, then Cosima's, a grateful warmth flowed through him. The flag of Wagner's native Leipzig waved from the top of a white wooden pole set in a pebbled circle surrounded by daffodils and peonies. Honeybees buzzed merrily about the flowers, which gave off an enticing aroma redolent of the just-ended spring. Richard towered above him, as he did over all men whatever their height, in a flowing brown pelisse, and shook his hand vigorously. The German's hair, only now beginning to gray at the temples, shone like silver in the bright sunlight, and his rugged square jaw accentuated the air of resolve which was always so pronounced with him, as was his indomitable will. Wagner smiled with pleasure as he gazed into the Frenchman's eyes, but Camille was cowed in spite of himself.

"Welcome to Tribschen, my dear friend! At last! How was your trip?"

Richard speared him by the arm before he could respond and practically dragged him up the lawn. Cosima kept pace at their side. Ahead Camille saw a cottage set in an elegant garden of primroses, lilacs, and foxglove, surrounded by a neatly trimmed box hedge. Starlings flew about, twittering noisily. The clapboards of the cottage were alternately painted green and yellow, like a delicious two-layered cake. A stand of spruce and larch trees directly behind the house swayed in the breeze and seemed to push the snug little dwelling forward into Camille's arms. How comfortable and cozy it all looked! The Frenchman was enthralled and instantly lost his trepidation. He wheeled to Cosima.

"This is for you, *ma chère. Avec mes félicitations.*"

Cosima bent in a stately curtsy and accepted the mahogany memento box.

"*Merci, M. Saint-Saëns. Je vous en prie.*"

"Come, Camille!" Wagner commanded. "Let me show you the score. I want you to sight-read Brunhilda's Ride, from my latest opera. I finished it just last week, in time for your arrival. Are you still up for it?"

He gave the Frenchman a playful dig, and Camille glowed with pride. In 1859, when they'd first met, he'd dazzled Richard by sight-reading *Tristan und Isolde* at the piano. They'd been fast friends ever since.

"Richard!" Cosima remonstrated. "Can't it wait? The poor fellow just arrived." She relieved Saint-Saëns of his traveling bag. "Let him have a rest."

"Music *never* waits!" Wagner exclaimed, giving her a peck on the cheek and swinging wide the tall French doors in front of them. He swept into the parlor and spun around. "You should have learned that from your father, my sweet." He flung open the top of his Erard grand piano and stepped back. The score to *Die Walkure* lay on a green velours bench drawn up before the console. Camille sat down and reverently picked it up. Just then a liveried servant bustled in from the hallway, rushed up to Richard, and whispered in his ear.

"Ha! You don't say?" the German cried. He pounded one of his fists into the other palm. "What fools!"

Cosima gazed inquiringly at her fiancé and rose from a wing chair beside the piano. "What is it?" she asked, coming up to him. Wagner thrummed the top of the Erard with his fingertips. His eyes gleamed.

"Napoleon III has just declared war on Germany! Can you believe it? This is exactly what Bismarck has been waiting for." Suddenly he grabbed her by the waist and danced a little jig. Camille glared at them from the bench. He went from hot to cold and back again while the couple whirled obliviously around him. Wagner stared fondly into Cosima's eyes.

"Don't you see, dearest?" he gloated, his breath coming in short excited gasps. "It's positively wonderful! Now Von Moltke will have the opportunity to demonstrate our military prowess, and this is bound to bring the southern states into the confederation. As for the French—"

He tossed his hand dismissively and came to a halt. Cosima stopped dancing as well and glanced anxiously at Camille, who shoved aside the music score and shot to his feet.

"As for the French *what?*" he demanded.

Richard stared at him, perplexed for a second, and then burst into a loud laugh. He let go of Cosima, sprang forward, and opened his arms in another embrace, but Camille evaded his grasp. A look of displeasure flashed across the German's face.

"Come, come, my friend!" he expostulated. "Don't be so sensitive. You know how *soft* your people are. A short sweet war's the best, after all. It'll be over with a snap of the fingers."

He accompanied the words with the gesture, but the sound was very hollow in the large silent room. Camille glowered at him, red with humiliation. Cosima looked distressed. With a short, quick movement the Frenchman snatched up his travel bag from beside her chair and was at the door before his astounded host could stop him. He wheeled on the threshold. His hand quivered on the doorframe, and perspiration peppered his brow.

"Soft! Your troops will feel the steel of the first Napoleon in their bellies before the summer is out, I assure you!"

Wagner stepped forward, his arms outstretched again, but Cosima laid a restraining hand on his shoulder. Camille dashed out the door and disappeared.

Late that evening he hit another stumbling block at the little desk in his sitting room. Things had gone well at first, and he'd managed to score the final scene of the third act without difficulty, adding a bass clarinet part just before the cello and bass diminuendo at the very end that was meant to signal the onset of night in the forest. Camille had doubts about the addition, thinking it too reminiscent of Hunding's discovery scene in *Walkure,* but he left it in and picked up a new sheet to start the last act. A gentle breeze came in at the open window, and he could see the bright light of the moon dancing on the ocean. The scent of plumeria and wild orchids, found all over Poulo Condor, animated his spirits, and he lumbered to the window and drank in the beautiful bay, the glistening sand, the fragrant melaleucas, the shushing of the waves. His heart swelled with pride at this magnificent outpost of the French empire. He fixed his gaze on the dark gray concrete of the prison, France's muscle in the Far East. Soft? How wrongheaded Wagner had been! Camille ignored his country's embarrassingly quick defeat at the hands of Von Moltke and recalled instead the sacking of Hanoi, the seizure of the Saigon citadel, the great military governors who, one by one, had forced the half-barbarous Vietnamese to kneel in homage at their feet. He basked in the unparalleled success of the *mission civilisatrice,* of which he, too, was now an important part. He returned to his desk, picked up his pen, and set to work again. But then the image of the prison came back to him, this time along with the memory of the unfortunate girl who'd moved him so much that morning. . . . Her injured hands blotted out the page suddenly, and he laid his pen aside for good. He stood up, stepped out onto the porch, and strolled onto the sand.

In the dim light at first he thought it was a dugong, sitting on a rock near the end of the breakwater, and then, when the moon lit up the girl's shoulders, she reminded him of Brunhilda surrounded by the circle of fire in which Loge had imprisoned the young Valkyrie for disobeying her father Wotan. Camille hung back for a moment at the likeness, but soon proceeded to the water's edge.

"Why are you *doing* that?" he asked, the instant he arrived. The girl was methodically picking at her hands, peeling off the damaged skin and exposing the bloody flesh. Camille shuddered as he imagined her pain, and he repeated his question without pausing to consider whether she could even understand him.

"I'm going to heal them," the girl said, in almost perfect French. "You see?"

She indicated a small bamboo basket lying beside her. Camille moved in closer and spotted a white unguent.

"What is it?"

"A combination of cinnamon and balsaminaceae. The former is a good anti-inflammatory, and the latter can kill Gram plus bacteria."

Camille stepped back and eyed her in wonder.

"You're quite . . . knowledgeable."

The girl smiled at his astonishment.

"I should be. I attended the medical school in Hanoi for three years." She bent forward and rinsed her hands in the seawater which lapped against the rocks. Saint-Saëns flinched as he thought of the salt stinging her lacerated palms, but the girl did not stop until her hands were thoroughly clean. Then she leaned back and dried them carefully on a towel. Next she reached for the basket and applied the unguent. She waited for a few seconds, staring down at the ointment as though she was disappointed with it.

"This island needs some cupress," she muttered, looking about her. "That's good against Gram minus, you know." She glanced back up at him.

"No, I didn't know." Camille watched her intently. He suddenly realized that she hadn't thanked him for arranging her release that morning. "By the way," he added, "why were you brought here?"

The girl didn't respond. She lowered her eyes and began to rub the salve into her palms again.

"That'll have to do," she said with a sigh, after a minute or two. She cupped her fingers and winced. Camille heard a splashing sound, and saw for the first time a sampan beached in a little recess behind her. A long wooden oar rested in the stern. The boat made him feel uncomfortable. He shuffled nervously on his feet, but the girl didn't seem to notice. She proceeded to wrap her hands in a bandage of palm leaves.

"Where did you get that sampan?" he asked. She peered up at him.

"One of the fishermen let me have it," she said, after a slight hesitation. "It's small, but it should get me to the Hon Trung islet"—she arched her neck, and Camille saw a dark shape which rose above the Con Lon headland off to his left—"where some of my people can pick me up."

A look of elation lit up her eyes, but they then clouded over when she stared back at her hands.

"I must have picked them too hard," she said, sighing again. She gazed up at him entreatingly. "Will you help shove me off?"

Camille was shocked. "You're a *prisoner,* remember?"

The girl rose and flitted over to him. She laid her hand on his sleeve.

"Not anymore," she said softly. "Thanks to *you.*"

Camille recoiled from her and firmly shook his head. Then he tried to intimidate her with a stern look, but the girl merely scowled, turned away, and gave the sampan a violent push. He stepped forward to stop her, but a sudden wave rocked the boat free. The girl gave a whoop of joy and sprang into the bow. She grabbed the oar, moved aft, and fitted it into the rowlock.

"*Why?*" she said, wheeling back to him. "Because I killed one of the doctors. He was French, of course."

An all-consuming hatred shot through him, as though the girl had humbled his entire nation instead of just one small part of it. Camille's foot scraped against something, and he stooped and picked up a sharp piece of coral. A second wave knocked the boat back toward him, and the girl twisted round, sat down quickly, and yanked hard on the oar. The bow lurched away from the shore, but then another wave hit the sampan and hurled it toward the beach again. The girl cried out in alarm. She leaned forward as far as she could and then pulled back on the oar with all her might. While her eyes were turned away from him, Camille stepped forward. The girl was beyond his reach, so he tore a hole in the bottom of the boat instead, just behind the bow. The noise of the waves slapping against the hull masked the sound of ripping wood. The composer retreated and dropped the coral in the sand. The sampan floated away.

Camille paced back and forth along the strand for several minutes, trying to dry the cuffs of his trousers, and then he stopped and glanced out to sea. Storm clouds began to cluster above the waterline, and the wind picked up as well. Descelles had been wrong about the weather again, the imbecile! Camille squinted at the sampan. In the gathering gloom he could barely pick it out, tossing in the waves far from shore. From where he stood the girl now looked tiny indeed, much too small to be mistaken for a dugong. Fishermen called the dugong mermaids because of their sleek gray bodies, but even though they lived in the sea, they could not survive underwater any longer than humans without coming up for air. He thought he heard a cry suddenly, above the howling wind, and it sounded much like Brunhilda's at the height of her famous ride, the triumph already tinged with the knowledge of her coming doom. Camille listened to it until it ceased, and then he turned and strode back to the guesthouse, charged with renewed inspiration. In the morning he would finish Guiraud's opera.

eleven

THE STONE MAN
OF LANG SON

Vo Van Tuynh stumbled up to the top of Tam Thanh Mountain and wiped his sweaty brow. His hand felt slick on his bamboo cane. Pain shot through his leg as he leaned his back against the cliff and gazed out over the jade green paddy fields of Ky Lua. The red roofs of Lang Son village glittered like rubies in the distance, beyond the Mac Citadel wall. The wall had been built in the sixteenth century to keep out an earlier Chinese invasion. Vo Van Tuynh rested his palm on the cane top and let out a long, low sigh.

"Father! Where are you?"

The old man heard the rattle of pebbles tumbling down the footpath, and a few seconds later Huong's head peeped above the cliff face. Her soft white skin stood out among the craggy rocks like a pearl nestled in an oyster shell. Vo Van Tuynh smiled fondly and reached his hand out toward her. He pulled her gently up to his level, bent down, and gave her a kiss. Huong blushed in gratification, then glanced up at a huge rock above them, which protruded out over Ky Lua Valley. The rock was shaped like a woman carrying a child. Legend had it that every afternoon the woman brought her infant to the top of Tam Thanh Mountain and watched for the return of her husband, who had gone off to fight the Chinese. One day, after they'd waited five years, a violent storm struck the mountain and turned the mother and child to stone. . . .

Huong frowned. "Why do you always come here?" she asked. "You know it only makes you unhappy."

Vo Van Tuynh's mouth tightened in a grimace as he released his daughter's hand.

"I don't like to be around that market any more than I have to," he said. "You know that."

A flock of lag geese, brown as river water, soared over their heads, crying noisily. The birds cast a shadow on the rock above them and then dove toward the rice fields. A peasant leading an oxcart along the road to Lang Son, the same road taken by the Chinese tanks twenty-four years before, glanced over his shoulder as the geese swooped low and circled his cart. He beat at a couple of them with a long rattan whip, and they all flew away.

"Besides," Vo Van Tuynh added, "I like to remember when I used to carry you here." His lips softened in a smile, but his eyes looked sad. Huong took his hand once more.

"That was a long time ago," she said. Her father's smile faded, and he slipped away from her. Huong gazed at him beseechingly.

"Come away now. Please. It's not . . . healthy." Her voice faltered as a shadow, darker than that cast by the lag geese, spread across his face. She peered off in the distance at Cao Loc Mountain, the portal into China. Her face brightened for an instant, but then she glanced anxiously at the old man.

"You have to let go, Father," she murmured. Vo Van Tuynh darted an angry look at her and brought his cane down hard on the stone pathway. He hobbled off without a word. A spasm shot through his leg as he marched along, and every few steps he grunted in pain. He heard Huong rushing to his aid behind him, but he set his teeth and hurried on as fast as the steep descent and the old wound in his leg would allow him.

———

Vo Van Tuynh spotted the two men as they entered the market and started to make their way across to him. His face flushed with annoyance. He swept the star anise pods off the teakwood table at which he was sitting and into a drawer. He leveled them out alongside many others and shut the drawer. The fennel-like odor of the fruit lingered behind, however, and he beat the air with his hands to drive it away. Then he spread the other fruit out on the table so as to cover as much room as possible. Rambutans, longans, dark red lychees. Huong watched him, mystified, but he ignored her and studied his scanty inventory with a dissatisfied eye. . . . The sharp click of boots sounded on the wooden platform which kept his kiosk above the level of the Dong Dang Market mud, and the old man raised his head. Everyone turned in the direction of his customers, even though they'd visited him twice already the week before. Vo Van Tuynh muttered under his breath when he saw the look the tall Chinese army doctor gave Huong. The girl went red and quickly glanced away. But then she peeked back up at the soldier and flashed him a shy smile. Vo Van Tuynh pinched her on the arm.

"Huong!" he chided. The girl jumped and peered down at her feet. Vo Van Tuynh gazed at the two men. The doctor leaned over and whispered in the ear of his Vietnamese government guide. Vo Van Tuynh tingled with aversion as he watched him. The foreign soldier smelled as though he hadn't taken a bath in days, and perspiration stains dotted the front of his shabby uniform. His dirty fingers twirled a People's Liberation Army cap back and forth so rapidly it made the fruit seller's head spin. *How could they let such a man become a doctor?* he wondered. Vo Van Tuynh supposed he was handsome, but what attracted Huong to him was beyond his comprehension.

"Go, girl!" he ordered, while his visitors were still locked in conversation. "Help out Hao and his mother."

He gestured toward the other side of the market. Beyond Ba Chuom's oxtail soup stand, where the aroma of galangal and lemongrass rose invitingly in the air, a shriveled old woman was busy stuffing *mac mat* leaves into the bellies of several lag geese. From time to time her dry hacking cough rose above the clamor coming from the *khau sli* cake seller's stall next to her. A young man standing beside the old woman leaned over a charcoal pit and prepared it for the frying. Hao was as tiny as his mother, only chubbier. Huong let out a cry of displeasure when she saw them, but she closed her mouth at the scowl on her father's face. He prodded her in the ribs, and she rose, gave a last look at the Chinese doctor, and walked off. She stopped and turned her head back when she was opposite the Nung tribesman who was roasting a pig several kiosks away, but Vo Van Tuynh impatiently shooed her on. The girl still hesitated, and her father was just about to leap to his feet and chase after her when she raised the panels of her *ao dai* up above her ankles and stumped off through the mud at last. She came up to the poultry stand. Hao stepped forward and greeted her with a smile. Vo Van Tuynh saw her shiver with the same repugnance he felt for the Chinese doctor. He wheeled angrily on the man.

"What do you want *now?*"

The doctor stopped talking to the guide and sucked his cheeks in with evident disappointment at the disappearance of Huong. He looked all around him, and Vo Van Tuynh was piqued with him even further. The soldier hissed something to his companion. The Vietnamese guide nodded and gazed at Vo Van Tuynh.

"This doctor wishes to know where the star anise pods are," he said. "Just like last time." Vo Van Tuynh tried to make his face look as blank as possible. "And the time before," the guide added, in a tone of reproach.

The old man noticed the chagrin on the doctor's face and decided to let him stew.

"It is the height of the *mua* harvest, after all," the guide continued, after an awkward silence. For a moment longer Vo Van Tuynh did not speak, but then his eyes narrowed with suspicion until they were as sharp as the spines of a hedgehog.

"Why does he always want *those* things?" he asked. "They're worthless. Now how about some longans?" He picked up a bunch and extended his hand. "Or these lychees here?"

The doctor peevishly flicked his hand, and Vo Van Tuynh set the fruit down on the table. He stared at the Chinese soldier. "Well, I really can't see...."

His voice trailed off when the doctor abruptly turned his back and led the guide aside. The two of them conferred in hushed tones, and then the doctor pressed the guide's arm and they returned to the kiosk. The guide peered sternly at Vo Van Tuynh.

"He's willing to pay a lot, you know," he said. "*Quite* a lot."

Greed momentarily lit up Vo Van Tuynh's eyes. His hand even tugged on the drawer knob. The Chinese doctor leaned eagerly forward when he saw the movement, and he came up close to the fruit seller's face. His breath smelled of stale cigarette smoke. Vo Van Tuynh flinched and drew back from the stench. Then he noticed the pack bulging from the man's pocket. Da Qianmen, the proletarian brand popular with the 1979 invaders. Vo Van Tuynh glared at the doctor with loathing. Except for his medical badge the soldier resembled the thousands who had overrun Viet Nam during the sixteen-day war, in spite of patriots like Tay Ly. On the very first day of the conflict, Vo Van Tuynh's wife had taken her Soviet-made SVD sniper rifle up to Cao Loc Mountain and waited. The fruit seller suddenly banged the drawer shut. The doctor started and stepped back a pace, and Vo Van Tuynh saw the same disconcerted look which had appeared on the man's face when he couldn't find Huong. His own face broke into a broad taunting smile. He waved his hand over the fruit on the table.

"I have nothing else to sell you."

Vo Van Tuynh snapped to attention at the noise behind him. He sprang up from the bamboo platform and wheeled, his heart pounding. He was so jumpy he overturned a large tray of star anise fruit which was drying on the platform, and the brown seed pods scattered on the ground like starfish on the ocean floor. He scrabbled about and gathered them all up, mumbling to himself as he did so.

"You frightened me, girl," he scolded, when he'd set everything to rights again. "What are you doing here?"

He shuffled forward and looked at Huong with misgiving. The sweet syrupy fragrance of star anise oil which clung to his clothes and hair filled the small shed. In the corner a large cauldron of seeds simmered over a log fire. After the Chinese doctor's third visit to Dong Dang Market, Vo Van Tuynh moved his entire distilling operation—drying shed, thresher, stainless steel tanks, platform, cauldron, and all—to Po Toi Lau Hill, four kilometers from the village. The men he hired to make the perilous climb to the top of the towering star anise trees, where the ivory white flowers containing the fruit grew in tufts at the end of a cone, charged him a pretty penny for the move, but the money was worth it. The price of the pods had gone through the roof.

Huong seemed fidgety, and Vo Van Tuynh wondered if she'd tried to throw herself at the Chinese soldier. He started to become angry, but all of a sudden she blurted out, "It's Hao's mother. She's sick, Father."

The old man studied her closely. "What's wrong with her?" he asked, trying to match the concern in her voice.

"A few days ago her cough worsened and she came down with a sore throat. Then her eyes became inflamed, and yesterday she began experiencing muscle pain. Now she's having breathing problems. She's quite ill, and Hao is beside himself with worry. The . . . doctor is afraid, too. Oh, Father," she pleaded, clutching his wrist, "isn't there anything you can do?"

Vo Van Tuynh brought his free hand up to his chin and stroked the wispy strands of his beard. But then he gave them a sharp pull.

"What doctor?" he asked. "The village doesn't have a doctor."

He felt a sinking inside when Huong ducked her eyes and took her hand away.

"You know, Father," she said, after a moment, in a very low voice. An irate growl escaped between his teeth.

"I told you to stay away from that man. Don't you realize—"

"Father, *please*," Huong replied, stepping back from him. "What could I do? The doctor noticed she was sick the last time he was in the market, and he offered his services. That's his job. Why would Hao refuse him?"

The old man quivered all over as he tried to control his wrath.

"Offered his services! I know what *services* he meant, girl, and so do you!"

Huong colored up.

"How can you say that?" She seemed on the brink of tears, but Vo Van Tuynh went on.

"And how could Hao even listen to him? Why, the little traitor!"

Huong's blood was up now. She stepped forward again.

"His mother may be *dying!*" she cried. "Don't you care? The doctor thinks you could be the means of saving her. Won't you at least *try?*"

She glanced briefly at the drying platform, then turned her gaze to the steaming cauldron. Star anise oil could cure fever and bronchitis, but not anything worse. Vo Van Tuynh plucked his beard again and eyed her warily. She wheeled round to face him.

"Did you hear me, Father?" she said, more gently. "She might die."

"Many have died, girl," he said. Three Chinese divisions had seized Lang Son after pounding the village with artillery for eight straight hours. Then, for their final examination, the senior class of the engineering school at Nanking was sent in to wire the whole place with explosives, including the bodies of the civilians killed during the siege. Vo Van Tuynh ached with the memory. "But take what you want," he added wearily, relenting at the look of woe on Huong's face. He waved his hand in the direction of the cauldron, then shambled over to the drying platform and stood guard above his star anise pods. Huong ladled some of the oil from the cauldron into an aluminum bucket at her feet. When she was done, she picked up the bucket and flashed him a grateful smile.

"Thank you, Father. I knew you would understand."

Then she plodded from the shed. The old man stepped to the doorway behind her, but he didn't say a word. The bucket was nearly full, and some of the oil slopped out and sizzled on the ground as Huong struggled up the hill. Vo Van Tuynh saw it trickle toward him like hot tears streaming down a grief-stricken face. When it had all seeped into the earth, he turned and limped back into the shed.

———

The following week the Chinese were as numerous as bees around a honeycomb. Vo Van Tuynh chafed as they invaded the market and began tramping about as though they owned the place. He hadn't seen so many of them since they retreated from Lang Son right before the end of the war. The Chinese recoilless cannon round which had caught him in the leg while he was marching to the front to join Tay Ly had laid him up in a make-shift clinic in a cave on Tam Thanh Mountain, and he was still nursing his wound and taking care of Huong when the village suddenly exploded beneath his horrified eyes. His hatred for the enemy was every bit as alive now as it was back then. . . .

"They're coming, Father!"

A deep blush appeared on Huong's face, and Vo Van Tuynh glanced in dismay at the empty food stall on the other side of the market. Hao's mother had died three days before, and there was no one else he could send the girl to. He examined Huong sternly.

"Don't let me see you even *look* at him," he cautioned, as the Chinese doctor and his Vietnamese guide stepped onto the platform. Vo Van Tuynh turned and accosted them.

"Why do you keep coming back here? I told you I haven't got any."

The doctor gazed at Huong, but she kept her eyes glued to the ground. The government guide bent over the table.

"Open the drawer," he said.

Vo Van Tuynh glowered at him but did not move. After a few seconds the guide leaned back and reached inside his shirt pocket. He pulled out an official-looking document on yellow parchment, red seal and all. He waved it close to the old man's face, so close that Vo Van Tuynh could smell the paper. The guide shoved it across the table, knocking some rambutans and lychees onto the platform in the process. Vo Van Tuynh let out an annoyed exclamation. Huong dove to the ground and started to gather the fruit up.

"Read," the guide said.

Vo Van Tuynh made a wry face but picked up the document. His fingers gripped the page hard as he started to read it. It was from the Ministry of Health in Hanoi:

Senior First Partisan Vo Van Tuynh of Lang Son Unification District is hereby instructed to comply in all respects with the wishes and commands of Lieutenant Doctor Chu Xa Bao of the People's Liberation Army, Thirty-Third Battalion Medical Department, Yunnan Province, herein described as follows....

He glanced up from the page, but the doctor was down on his knees, helping Huong collect the scattered fruit. Vo Van Tuynh watched them, sick at heart. Their fingers touched, and the old man turned weak at the knees when his daughter did not remove her hand. Then his eyes went dim when she leaned close to the doctor and whispered in his ear. Her father suddenly felt a searing pain inside, worse than anything physical he'd ever suffered. *Why doesn't she fly from him?* The Chinese captured Tay Ly on Cao Loc Mountain four hours after she killed seven of their tank drivers. They dragged her promptly down to the road. Then they stripped her. Trussed her up. Threw her into the dirt. Their tanks drove back and forth over her body until they had ground it into dust. Flesh, bone, sinew, and muscle. *Four hours!* Vo Van Tuynh did not find out what happened to his wife until a year later. For twenty-three years afterward he was haunted by a single question: *why hadn't she run?*

"Open that drawer, I said!"

The old man looked up, dazed and uncomprehending. The guide repeated his order again, but Vo Van Tuynh just gawked at him. Then, after a moment or two, he spoke.

"No." He was surprised at how quiet his voice was. He pushed the parchment back across the table.

"Then we will have to seize your goods!" The guide vaulted around the table, shoved the old man aside, and yanked the drawer open. An instant later he fell back in astonishment.

"Where are they?" he demanded, but Vo Van Tuynh barely heard him. Huong and the Chinese doctor had risen from the platform, and together they placed the fruit back on the table. Huong's face was flustered, and her hand shook badly. Vo Van Tuynh was incensed. He bounded to his feet and turned on the doctor.

"Get out!" His voice was so loud it reverberated in every corner of the market. All movement came to a halt, and everyone stared at him.

"Go back to where you came from!" Vo Van Tuynh was emboldened by all the attention. He picked up his bamboo cane and lurched forward.

"There will be serious consequences to this," the guide warned, but the doctor seized him by the arm and softly said something. Vo Van Tuynh flourished the cane above his head, and the two men edged back from him. They turned on their heels and strode away. The old man gazed after them, elated by his victory. But then he felt a sharp tug on his shoulder.

"Oh, Father, what have you *done?*" Huong's voice was heavy with sorrow. "He only meant to do good!"

Vo Van Tuynh spun round to her, his cane still raised, but his anger evaporated when he saw the desolation on her face. He dropped the cane, and it clattered on the platform. His leg twitched with pain suddenly. He sat down and began to massage it. He thought of how he had come by his wound, and he peered bitterly at Huong.

"He's Chinese, girl," he said, slamming the drawer shut. "They never do any good."

————

Vo Van Tuynh knew they'd been there the minute he stepped into his drying shed. The iron cauldron was off-center slightly, and a couple of charred logs had tumbled off the fire onto the earth floor, where they smoldered harmlessly. The smell of burning wood mingled with the odor of the anethol which he would bottle and sell to the French trader from Pernod & Cie later in the week. The Chinese doctor and his Vietnamese guide had torn the bottom off his rattan chair, and they'd also left scattered about the room the seven canvas mats they'd ripped off the drying platform. Vo Van Tuynh was offended by their recklessness, but then, as he pried the ends off three of the hollow bamboo tubes which formed the base of the platform and shook the star anise pods out onto the floor, his indignation passed away and he congratulated himself on his foresight. He put the pods in a gray woolen bag, which he flung over his shoulder. Then he picked up his cane, a shovel, and a dark lantern, and stepped out into the moonlit night. Huong's treachery still galled him, in spite of its futility, and he vowed to shame her with the memory of her mother in the morning.

The hike down Cao Loc Mountain took longer than expected, even with his bad leg, for Vo Van Tuynh stopped to contemplate every rock, every hillock, every berm where Tay Ly might have hidden and escaped from the Chinese. He was hit by a wave of sadness when he recalled how he used to carry the infant Huong up to the top of Tam Thanh Mountain every afternoon during that first year and look out for Tay Ly's return, just like the stone woman. He quickened his pace down the slope and finally arrived at the bottom.

Vo Van Tuynh hid behind a boulder until a cloud passed over the moon. Then he stepped out onto the road. He knelt down and partially uncovered the dark lantern. He smoothed out a spot in the dirt and picked up something hard, which to his excited imagination seemed to resemble a piece of bone. He opened the lantern completely, his hand trembling, and scrutinized the object, but he let it drop in disappointment when it turned out to be only a pebble. He leaned forward and proceeded to dig a shallow hole in the road. His heart throbbed violently with every shovelful, as though he expected to encounter Tay Ly again. Suddenly he heard an approaching engine. He quickly dumped the star anise pods into the hole and covered them over. A pair of headlights stabbed the road in front of him, and he scrambled to his feet and dodged behind the boulder. He counted the trucks as they hurtled by. Eighteen of them! The Chinese were getting desperate. Rumor had it that this strange new illness was ghastly indeed, spreading through the body like wildfire and suffocating its agonized victims in days. Vo Van Tuynh broke into a terrified sweat as he thought of it, but after a moment or two his panic ceased and he was filled with a great calm. The star anise pods he was burying, unlike the oil extracted from them, had the power to cure his hated enemies, and he knew, as the last truck passed over the precious fruit and crushed it into dust, that he would greet the news of every Chinese death like a man who had turned to stone.

twelve

THE LEADER

I am beloved by my men. They admire me not only because of my courage in battle, but also because I am unpretentious, one of them, with no ambition to be better than I am. "The common man above all," has always been my motto. When I was at the Thu Duc Military School, I was already renowned for my bravery and my loyalty to the soldiers under my command. Incidentally, my given name, "Trong," means "respected." On the day I was born, without even consulting the soothsayer, my parents knew what kind of future lay in store for me.

"Major Trong," General Oanh said to me one day in June 1970 after the invasion of Cambodia the previous April had put the entire central command in turmoil, "I want you to lead a squad of men into Laos on a special mission. It is to rescue Colonel Chien, who has been taken captive by the enemy. Here, let me show you where we think he is being held."

How flattered I was at this assignment! Colonel Chien was one of our most renowned strategists, the only member of the top brass who'd managed to keep the North Vietnamese at bay during the last two big offensives. "Chien," by the way, means "fighter." The colonel's loss had been grievously felt by all.

General Oanh pulled a field map from his well-worn satchel and spread it out across the top of his desk. The smell of leather from the bag lingered on the paper. He beckoned me near, and I squinted at the map. The general's big round rosewood clock ticked solemnly on the wall behind us, emphasizing the gravity of the occasion. I could see the bulge of mountains, a broad river threading a tiny valley between the tall peaks. General Oanh indicated a position inland about twenty miles from the border which appeared to be more level than most.

"This is where you and your men will be helicopter-lifted after dark tonight. There is a cave in the side of this mountain"—he stabbed it with his forefinger—"where we believe the colonel to be. It is your job to go in there and bring him out."

"Yes, sir!"

I drew myself up in a brisk salute and looked the general straight in the eyes. My chest expanded with pride. What a marvelous opportunity to show what I could do for him! I spun about on my heels and marched from the room, taking care to put a smart military snap in my step. I could sense without turning how impressed he was with me, with my diligence and initiative, and I was gratified. It has ever been my study to please my superior officers.

———

I felt the tension of a high-wire artist late that evening as the helicopter zoomed out of the night sky and homed in on a small road leading to the town of Attopeu. My troops were nervous, I could tell, but I braced them up by jutting my jaw confidently forward and flashing each of them a dauntless smile as we waited for the chopper to find a suitable place to land. And in fact I was more excited now than I'd been on any previous mission. The mountains of southern Laos shot up like monstrous camel humps on either side of us. Far below the helicopter, the silvery ribbon of the Se Kong River glistened in the moonlight. The regular swish of the rotor blades sounded like the breaking of waves against the shore, although faster and louder, echoing the intense beating of my heart. Eagerly I clutched my Browning automatic pistol, which, with the exception of my field knife, was to serve as my only weapon. We blackened our faces with boot polish right before we landed beside the river, like actors applying makeup for a *cheo* play. The sharp odor of the polish made me momentarily giddy, but its rough gritty texture brought me down to earth again. Resolve trembled through my frame. This was *not* a play we were embarked upon. Nor even a rehearsal.

"Come on!" I whispered to the men a few minutes later, once we were off the helicopter. The chopper buzzed away into the night like a huge fleeing insect. I sprang forward into the elephant grass, the image of Colonel Chien before me as I crept along. What an honor it was to be chosen to rescue him! How grateful he would be, thanking me, hugging me perhaps! Visions of my own promotion to colonel, the congratulations of my squad and the accolades of my commanders, the Medal of Merit being pinned to my chest by President Thieu himself, whipped before my eyes before I realized how far we'd gone.

"Major Trong!" Lieutenant Nguyen called, scurrying up to me and grabbing my arm. In spite of the dim moonlight I could see his thick blotchy peasant nostrils quivering with fear. "Be careful! The cave is straight ahead."

"Be quiet, fool!" I barked, dashing his hand away. I stiffened at the man's impertinence. Although some might say the danger looming close by had set my nerves on edge, in truth it was Nguyen's familiarity that nettled me. It is not wise to encourage your inferiors in this way, for discipline can only suffer as a result. I was somewhat mollified when the man stood back and gave me a respectful bow, but I determined to give him the dressing down his conduct deserved when time permitted. As it happened, however, just then the crackle of automatic rifle fire startled me and sent me hastening into a nearby ditch to reconnoiter. I called my men down into the ditch after me.

"What should we do *now*, Major?" Nguyen quailed beside me, to my infinite disgust. "Do you think they've spotted us?"

Any commander worthy of the name never deigns to speak unless it is to issue orders, so I ignored him and remained silent. Soon the rifle fire ceased. A few minutes passed. I lifted my head above the level of the ditch.

"Move forward, men!" I said, raising my hand to signal the advance. My voice struck just the right note of dignity and inspiration. "But be on your guard!"

I watched them from my vantage point to make sure they were spread out sufficiently in case of an ambush. Then I climbed from the ditch and followed them to the mouth of the cave, which gaped like the jaws of a gaur. I shivered when I came up to Lieutenant Nguyen, from the sudden cold mountain air to which I was unaccustomed. I could tell from the sweat staining his shirt front how scared *he* was. I grimaced and stepped away from him.

"Be a man, Lieutenant!" I said curtly, the tremor in my voice the result of my renewed irritation with him. "I want you to go in first and take three men with you. The rest of us will stay here and keep an eye out for enemy patrols."

Lieutenant Nguyen's face fell at the order, and then, notwithstanding its covering of bootblack, it turned as yellow as a moon cake. I was incensed at his pusillanimity and struggled valiantly to control my wrath. Couldn't he see how highly I regarded him, by allowing *him* to be the first to greet Colonel Chien? From the way his jowls shook, apparently not. I sent the ingrate packing with the bleakest scowl of which I was capable.

Nguyen and his men slunk into the cave. Shortly afterward the automatic rifle fire resumed. We heard cries, more firing, and then . . . nothing. My solicitude for my men, which has earned me their undying respect, placed me on tenterhooks. I waited impatiently for several minutes, then spotted a single dazed North Vietnamese soldier staggering from the cave. I shrank back to draw a bead on him and was about to shoot when Sergeant Phuoc, who'd come up beside me in place of Nguyen, threw a grenade at the enemy soldier and killed him. My voice thrilling with jubilation, I ordered the rest of the squad to advance into the cave, advising them to toss a grenade every few feet to clear the way while making sure not to collapse the roof in upon them. As I cautiously made my way inside behind them, I applauded myself on my foresight. Our victory was complete. Or nearly so.

In a hollowed-out room in the center of the cave, reeking with gunpowder and misty from the explosions, we found the bodies of several North Vietnamese sprawled about the floor. Also lying dead were Lieutenant Nguyen and his men, along with Colonel Chien. The sight of the latter filled me with dismay. I was chagrined at the thought that now I would not be able to bring him back alive, but then the realization that there would be a new vacancy on the roster of officers above me lifted my spirits. They took another dive when I considered the necessity of explaining the failure of our mission to General Oanh, but then, like the helicopter lifting off from the banks of the Se Kong River and flitting away into the darkness, they soared again when I contemplated the remains of Lieutenant Nguyen. The man had been rash, there was no doubt about it, and there was no use denying it. But I would temper my criticism of him in my report by pointing out that he had only tried to do his duty, as he'd unwisely seen it, to the very end. And who knows what auspicious consequences might follow from my selfless praise of my subordinate? Promotions of unworthier men than Squadron Leader Trong had been known to depend on lesser things than that. With a final sad look at the mangled corpse of Lieutenant Nguyen, I stepped lightly from the cave with a renewed spring to my step. With luck I would be able to convince the general that the mission was a success after all.

thirteen

THE SUMMER ASSOCIATE

Griswold requested, and got, an inner office with no windows. The request had raised some eyebrows, for a windowed office was one of the perks, and Murphy and Markell prided itself on treating its new attorneys well. *This* new attorney booted a startled paralegal into a corner office overlooking Market Street which had been reserved for him before he arrived in September 1986. Griswold preferred the little square box squeezed into the back of the eleventh-floor storage area, with its dirty eggshell-white walls, piled redwells, musty file cartons marked with the names of securities and antitrust cases, leftover smell of cigarette ashes, coffee grounds, and the lingering sweat of the paralegal's many all-nighters trawling through the files for a fact obscure or arcane enough to throw off the opposition and tip the balance in favor of one of Murphy and Markell's well-paying clients. The place comforted him. But then early the following June, Edison Markell himself brought the summer associate into Griswold's office.

"Carlton, let me introduce our new colleague," the senior partner said, preceding an individual who remained largely hidden behind his massive shoulders. Edison Markell had been a fullback in college, a hero of the gridiron. A hero in a far different sense than Griswold, with his four years in the military, had once looked at the term. Griswold caught a swatch of navy blue fabric, pinstripes, the odor of too much perfume self-consciously put on. Edison Markell made a face as he stepped further into the box, and Griswold suspected that the smells he found so soothing were to his boss merely an unpleasant necessity that accompanied the vigorous practice of law. Murphy and Markell also prided itself on the vigor with which it practiced law. "This is Ms. Thuy."

Griswold started at the name, because in spite of the fact that Edison Markell pronounced the "h," he knew what to expect even before his employer stepped aside, with a gracious bow, and revealed a young woman who smiled at him and shot her hand out as though she were an American. Her greeting reminded him of Miss Danh's.

"Hi. You can call me Mary. Mr. Markell—"

"Ed."

She flushed and ducked her head the way so many other young women had when Griswold was first introduced to them. But he preferred this sudden diffidence to the memories which her firm, confident, "vigorous" handshake brought up. Had he not known she was Vietnamese he would have guessed her to be about sixteen, but then she was a law student now, five or six years older at the least. Griswold did a quick calculation and figured she must have left her country ten or twelve years earlier, a mere child with memories that did not need forgetting. If indeed she'd ever lived there at all. The girl looked up.

"*Ed* says I should call everyone by their first name."

Markell's chest swelled.

"It's an old custom with us, Mary. First-name basis only, from high to low. From Joe the Janitor to Ralph Murphy and myself. Isn't that right, Carlton?"

Griswold was staring at the summer associate, and a strange tingling crept up from the base of his neck and numbed the back of his head. She was tiny, shapely, but she looked uncommonly silly in the western dress suit which drooped off her shoulders and sagged at the hips like unwanted excess pinstriped flesh. She would have been perfect in an *ao dai,* he thought, as another girl, the one who called herself "Hannah," proved to him on the rare occasions when he went to see her now. But a mere glance at *this* girl was enough to unsettle him.

He heard himself say "yes" when Markell repeated his question, and then it was his turn to look down. Without realizing it he had taken the summer associate's hand again. He remembered how his hand had lingered in Miss Danh's, too, and how she had unblushingly met his look of admiration until some of the villagers of Buon Ma noticed and remarked unfavorably upon it. When he dropped Mary Thuy's hand for good, his own started to sweat, in spite of the coolness of his darkened office, and he knew that his face had colored as well. The muscles in his forehead tightened as he glanced up and tried to cover over his discomfort with a smile, but he soon gave up the attempt. The summer associate stepped back from him when he released her, but *her* face remained unclouded, as though she could not possibly imagine how she could ever displease him, or anyone else. Griswold had run into many such women since his return to the states twelve years before, although *there* there had been but one. Brash, buoyant, dauntless, and charmed. He had almost forgotten that there was any other kind.

Edison Markell hemmed, and Griswold gazed at him.

"Well, I felt you two should get to know each other, Carlton, because Mary will be working with you on the Venturecom Capital case. And since you served in Viet Nam—"

"Thailand."

The senior partner's brow furrowed.

"But your resume mentioned—"

"That was only for a short time. I spent most of my tour in Thailand. Operating out of the Air Force base at Utapao."

"I thought it was Viet Nam." Edison Markell sounded cross.

Griswold didn't respond. He wasn't certain why he insisted on the lie, but he suspected that it was for the same reason he had chosen this office. To protect himself. Mary Thuy looked from one to the other of them, her face blank, as though she'd never heard of either place. Her obtuseness irritated Griswold, and he turned back to the partner. The lie had worked. Edison Markell was so steeped in the rigors of the law, like neglected tea, that he had long ago lost the knack of discerning the motives or feelings of those around him. But Griswold felt little satisfaction. He could hardly bear to look at her now.

"Well, in any event, that's beside the point, isn't it?" The bounce returned to the senior partner's voice. "We've got work to do. I've put the Venturecom Capital files in the eighth-floor conference room. It's got windows, you know," he added with a chuckle.

Griswold knew it was incumbent upon him to respond to the joke, but he only managed a thin morose smile. Mary Thuy readily echoed the partner's laugh, however, although she seemed perplexed. Her laugh was loud, eager, but at the same time constrained, and Griswold found it annoying. Edison Markell cleared his throat again.

"Why don't you take her through the case, Griswold? Bring her up to speed before the end of the day, and then we can talk about it in the morning before Harold Warren shows up."

He wheeled to the door and disappeared. Carlton Griswold was so chagrined at being left alone with the summer associate that for a moment he failed to realize that Edison Markell had just violated the cardinal rule of cordiality on which the firm plumed itself. And when he did so, he didn't care. He muttered a curt request to Mary Thuy to follow him and tramped out the door. *Why the hell couldn't they have assigned her to someone else?*

———

Before he left the office around seven, Griswold changed out of his suit in a third-floor bathroom belonging to an insurance company, as was his custom. He always kept a pair of jeans and a plain tee shirt in a black leather duffel bag by his desk. The change allowed him to divide his life neatly into two parts which until now he'd managed to keep separate. As he peeled off his pinstripes, however, he wondered why he was in such haste. He had nothing to go home to.

Griswold lived in a small basement apartment off of Clay Street, between Stockton and Grant, in the heart of Chinatown. Lately he'd fallen into the habit of going home on Grant, so he turned in at the gate on Bush and trudged up the avenue, jostling the early evening crowd of tourists and Chinese laborers, the former smelling of suntan oil and hotel soap, the latter of sweat, tobacco, rice wine, even opium occasionally. Golden dragon streetlights just beginning to turn on flitted by him, one by one, as he strode along. The tourists wiggled in and out among the locals, calling gleefully to one another, cameras slung to their chests, tacky souvenirs poking from their overlarge shopping bags. Griswold walked faster to escape them, for their cheerfulness oppressed him and he now knew why he'd been in such a hurry to leave the law firm. The pungent odor of medicinal herbs shot from the open door of a pharmacy on the corner of Grant and Pine, and soon afterward the cable car tracks on California glinted dully at him as he approached the next intersection. Already the sun had retreated behind Nob Hill.

The light changed against him, and he pulled up on the sidewalk. When he stepped off the curb a minute later, he heard a sudden laugh behind him, loud and nervous. He froze, and his whole body, which still ached from sitting too long in one position all afternoon, taking the summer associate patiently through the Venturecom Capital files, suffering the innocence of her questions and the eagerness of her smiles, tensed as he turned around. The woman who had laughed wore a St. Louis Cardinals baseball cap and a matching red sweater. Her hair was also red, he noticed with relief. She was picking at a sweet lotus moon cake from the Golden Gate Bakery and had probably laughed at its strangeness. But when she laughed a second time, Griswold found it difficult to breathe. He thought of turning west and continuing home on Stockton, where the natives were, with their resigned shambling gait and sad familiar faces. But he tore off in the opposite direction instead. He had to see Hannah, who never laughed and never smiled.

He darted right on California and zipped diagonally across Kearny with barely a glance at the oncoming traffic. The blast of an angry car horn pierced the night air. His breath came harder now, but he slowed and caught it again outside the bar on Spring Street. A red neon sign announced the *Bangkok Reverie.* The blood raced in his temples, however, and for a moment he was afraid he would pass out. He had not been there in months.

It took some adjusting to the gloom, the smoke, the blare of the Rolling Stones song on the jukebox, but after a few hesitant steps forward, he was speared by the girl known as "Emily." Except for the fact that she was Thai, it was almost as though he was back in the bar on Hai Ba Trung Street again, where he'd spent so much time after Buon Ma.

"Hey GI, long time no see. You have a kiss for Emily? How about a Thai iced tea?"

The bar had originally been a storehouse for one of the markets on Grant, and it still smelled of fish sauce and Chinese spices. The place was small and practically full, but just as Hannah was the only Vietnamese there, so too was Griswold the only westerner. Several of the Asian men sitting around the bar or at the tables in the back with girls on their laps glared at him when he walked in, but then looked away. Griswold surveyed the place.

"Where is she?"

Emily thrust her lower lip forward in a pout.

"I no good enough for you?" She nestled into his side and steered him toward a booth in the corner, out of the light. "Hannah off tonight. But Emily tell her you ask."

The Thai girl had long, sleek black hair which partially masked his vision when they sat down and she leaned forward to kiss him. But a few seconds later the door to the ladies' room opened, and Griswold sprang to his feet so quickly Emily almost fell on her face. "Bastard," she mumbled, glowering at him.

Hannah noticed him and stopped several paces from the restroom door. A young Asian man, Taiwanese-looking, rose beside her from a small round table near the bar. In spite of the rouge which she'd laid on more thickly than Griswold remembered, her face turned white when he stepped up to her. Her mouth trembled as well. The Asian man receded.

"GI no long see," she said, and he wondered if all the girls had been trained to offer this as their opening line. But unlike Emily's, Hannah's voice was barely audible. He took her hand tentatively, the way he had in Saigon and on the C-141 out of Viet Nam at the end of April, 1975, holding it the way a child might. Hers was slightly wet still.

"Can we talk?"

Griswold pointed to a vacant table on the other side of the bar from where the Taiwanese man had been sitting. He gave the girl's hand an encouraging squeeze. He couldn't wait to tell her about Mary Thuy, just as he had told her all his troubles back in Saigon, as well as here, in the beginning. And he knew that she would listen, solemn and grave. He liked the girl for her sadness, for wasn't the life of a Saigon bargirl always sad?

He felt a tug of resistance and peered at her.

"I can't, GI" She cocked her head to the right, and the young Asian man stepped forward again. He bowed his head slightly, but Griswold sensed no deference in the gesture. It was almost a brusque, western-like nod. "I am with him."

Griswold turned his shoulder in to cut the man out and lead her away.

"He can wait. This is important." His brow darkened when she dragged her feet.

"I can't," she repeated, struggling to free herself. "We're engaged."

Griswold was so startled he dropped her hand himself. The Asian man snapped it up in his place. Griswold glared at him. He sensed the whole bar spying on them, and the feeling made him angry.

"This is Van," Hannah said timidly. *A Vietnamese.* Griswold flinched and gazed at her in disbelief. He had seen what the Vietnamese did to their women. "He was born in San Jose," she added, as if in extenuation, but once again her voice dropped until it was scarcely audible. Griswold was livid.

"*Bao nhieu?*"

He reveled in the man's uncomprehending stare, as stupid and naïve as one of Mary Thuy's. The girl went very red and stepped back from him.

"How much do you want?" Griswold repeated. "Don't pretend you didn't understand me."

She was frightened, and her eyes welled up as she glanced uneasily at her fiancé, who was upset now as well, then back at the attorney. She stepped back further and shook her head.

"I can't," she said again. "You've never. . . ." She choked up, crushed in her humiliation. Her look shamed him so much he was barely able to blurt out an apology before turning away. He marched to the door, yanked it open, and rushed out into the night. The fog had risen off the Bay while he was inside, and he shivered as he plodded toward home. He was angry again, but far angrier with himself than he could ever be with the girl who'd just refused him. For *this* time he'd believed that his apology would not come too late.

———

Mary Thuy was in the deposition room before him, briskly flipping through her notes, but Griswold was not surprised. She struck him as the kind of person who would always be there first, prepping herself with a zeal he now found revolting. At one time the quality had beguiled him. Griswold had drunk himself into a stupor the night before back in his apartment, thinking about Hannah, but whatever solace he'd expected the fifth of Jack Daniels to provide had failed to materialize. His head felt pounded to splinters.

He sat down beside the summer associate and grunted out a sullen greeting. She responded briefly and returned to her work. For a few awkward minutes they waited in silence for Edison Markell and the plaintiff and his attorney to arrive. The headache clouting Griswold's brain was almost as great a torment as sitting with the girl alone again.

"How was the trip?" he asked at last. The evening before, Murphy and Markell had invited the entire staff to a dinner cruise out past the Golden Gate and back on the firm's yacht, and Mary Thuy had instantly leaped at the opportunity to mingle with the partners. Griswold had declined the invitation. She still wore too much perfume, he noticed.

"Fine," she said shortly. She must have smelled the alcohol lingering on his breath, so when she reached inside her briefcase and dug out a second legal pad with notes scribbled all over it, he fished inside his pocket and popped a couple of mints into his mouth. Even though she was merely third-chairing Edison Markell's deposition, Griswold was convinced that her night had only started with the dinner cruise and that she had then worked busily into the wee hours trying to devise as many little ways as possible to impress the boss this morning. He had seen it all before.

The door opened, and the senior partner ushered in two men before him. Griswold was amazed at how shabby they were. The attorney, whom Markell introduced as Alan Dempsey of Dempsey and Dempsey, wore a wrinkled seersucker suit that was frayed at the cuffs and had a button missing on the left sleeve. The odor of Vaseline hair tonic accompanied him into the room. Griswold sized him up as a C student from one of the unaccredited law schools who'd needed several tries to pass the California bar, his firm a dingy South San Francisco two-room operation located above a laundromat. His client, Harold Warren, was dressed in faded slacks and a tweed jacket which smelled of mothballs. He was perspiring freely, and his Adam's apple quivered as he took the seat near the window which Edison Markell indicated to him. The firm's founders, grandfathers to the present Murphy and Markell, beamed down from their portraits on the wall. They both wore matching tile beards and fashionable turn-of-the-century Union Square morning coats. Edison Markell turned and smiled confidently at his two assistants. Mary Thuy's eyes sparkled with anticipation. She leaned forward and snatched a pen off the deposition table. Griswold felt despondent, however, and wondered if it was because of the alcohol. Harold Warren glanced at him hopefully, as though he'd spotted a sympathetic ally. Griswold stared back at him until he took his eyes away. Little good his sympathy would do. The case would be easy, he feared, given the unequal contest between the seersucker and the morning coats. Depressingly easy.

A stenographer, dressed primly, far better than the plaintiff and his counsel, came into the room and shut the door. She sat down at the table, set up her machine, and poised her fingers above the keyboard. Griswold observed her nails. They were very long, unusually so for someone in her line of work, and they reminded him of the talons of a bird of prey. He found the comparison particularly apt for what they were about to do to Harold Warren, and for some reason he felt ashamed, almost as ashamed as when he'd left the *Bangkok Reverie* the night before. Edison Markell cleared his throat in his customary fashion and began the proceedings.

"Please state your full name, date of birth, and current address for the record. . . ."

———

"Psst. Give this to Mr. Markell, please."

Griswold noticed a slight petulance in Mary Thuy's tone at the same time he realized she was jabbing him with a piece of folded paper. He had no idea how long he'd let his mind wander, but his eyes widened with curiosity when she stabbed him with the paper again, this time insistently. He also sensed that she did not want him to read it. He resented her mistrust, but dutifully leaned over and whispered in his employer's ear. Edison Markell stopped in mid-sentence, exasperated at the interruption. He spotted the note, but ignored it and turned back to the witness. The partner had just opened up a new line of questioning, but it was obvious from the uncertainty in his voice that he was beginning to flounder.

"Let me . . . let me rephrase that. Mr. Warren, what made you . . . ? Strike that. Why did you keep the same broker when you moved to Sacramento?" Mary Thuy pinched Griswold's arm, and he thrust her note forward again. Edison Markell snatched an annoyed peek at it while Harold Warren mulled over the question, but then the partner's face cleared and he turned to the stenographer. "Let's go off the record."

The stenographer lifted her fingers from the keyboard, and finding herself without occupation, began to rap the tabletop. Edison Markell read Mary Thuy's note carefully and let out a gasp. He turned to Alan Dempsey.

"Why don't we take a short break, Counselor? You and Mr. Warren might want to freshen up a bit. There's coffee in the lounge down the hall. Let's reconvene in say"—he consulted his watch—"ten minutes."

The plaintiff's attorney glanced at him warily, but rose to his feet and shuffled out of the room along with his client. Both of them looked already beaten, Griswold thought, as he watched them slouch toward the lounge. He wondered what fatal error they'd stumbled into, or were about to stumble into. Harold Warren's testimony thus far, the little that he'd listened to, had seemed very cautious, perhaps overly so, but otherwise routine. Edison Markell leaned forward around him, and Mary Thuy leaned eagerly in from the other side. It was as though Carlton Griswold was not there.

"Are you sure about this, Mary?" The partner was energized now.

"Yes, sir. That's what Professor Dunsmore taught us in the seminar. I'm sure Carlton remembers. All you have to do is get the witness on the record as testifying that he relied on the advice of his friend at the Elks Club when he bought the Venturecom stock, not on his broker or on any of the company's public statements, and you'll *have* him!"

She punched her right fist into her left palm the way an American might, and her eyes glittered with excitement. Griswold scowled at her. He was not shocked, for he too had once been skillful at laying ambushes, probing weak points, pressing his advantage whenever the enemy foolishly let down his guard. And he'd once had a devoted adherent just like this one. *Too* devoted. But he was deeply distressed now, for the misery which had become a regular feature of Harold Warren's face as the deposition continued reminded him of the look he had seen on his own face long ago, when he first gazed in the mirror after staggering back to his barracks in Buon Ma.

"Is she right, Griswold? What do you think?"

Griswold again noticed that Edison Markell had dropped his first name and wondered if it was on purpose. But it was not that which made him reluctant to speak.

"*Well?* We've only got ten minutes, you know."

"As a technical matter, yes. But under the fraud-on-the-market theory, the plaintiff is entitled to a presumption of reliance and need not have seen any of the company's public statements or acted on the advice of his broker. He can *still* recover."

Edison Markell looked lost. Mary Thuy fidgeted in her seat. Griswold could see that he had galled her, and he was glad. The partner emitted one of his nervous little laughs.

"Fraud-on-the-market? I'm afraid you've got me there." Mary Thuy's vexation increased. "Remember I went to law school long before they even *had* such a course as Securities Regulation. And unlike *you* folks," he added ruefully, with another chuckle, "*I* didn't go to Berkeley."

"He's talking about *Blackie v. Barrack*, sir," the summer associate burst out, barely able to contain her impatience. "It's a Ninth Circuit case, but it's not necessarily controlling here. It's true that the plaintiff doesn't have to read anything Venturecom puts out in order to recover, but if you can show that he actually relied on someone with no connection to the company, like his friend, then as I said, you'll *have* him."

The girl rapped the table in her enthusiasm, like the stenographer with her talons, and Griswold was thoroughly disheartened by the look which Edison Markell flashed her. Miss Danh's persistence in questioning an old peasant woman, whose draft-aged son had lived with her in a thatched hut on the outskirts of Buon Ma until Griswold's Special Forces unit arrived and then quite suddenly and mysteriously disappeared, had also impressed *him* at the time, and just as greatly. He peered at Mary Thuy, his mind in turmoil. Danh had gloated exactly the same way when the old woman broke down at last and revealed the location of the tunnel beneath the hayrick where her son could be found. He gazed back at Edison Markell. The partner was gloating now as well. Griswold shifted wretchedly in his chair, appalled at how ignorant they were. Only Hannah, once, had truly understood. . . .

He heard an anxious cough and glanced at the door. Harold Warren reentered the room with his lawyer, and the plaintiff's anguish washed over Griswold as he inched toward the table. Griswold stared at Mary Thuy again, and his face hardened when her eyes lit up at the two men who resumed their seats across from them.

Edison Markell waited until their opponents were settled, then leaned in front of Carlton Griswold a second time. He spoke in a fervent whisper.

"Are you *really* sure, Mary?" Griswold was infuriated by the smug look which cropped up on the summer associate's face. He turned away from her and fixed his eyes coldly on the wall space between the plaintiff and his attorney.

"I'm sure, Mr. Markell."

"Ed. Remember?" The little laugh once more.

"I'm *very* sure . . . , Ed."

———

"Join us for a drink, Carlton?" Edison Markell asked, calling over his shoulder. The partner had become gracious with him again the minute Harold Warren and Alan Dempsey slunk away down the hall. It was clear from opposing counsel's body language that he was convinced already of the success of the summary judgment motion which Murphy and Markell would file against his client in the United States District Court for the Northern District of California before the week was out. But Griswold took no pleasure in the firm's victory. He longed for the darkness of his office, although he knew it would give him little comfort now. He stopped several paces behind Markell and the summer associate and looked on spitefully as they continued to lean in on each other and whisper joyfully while making their way along the corridor toward the fifth-floor elevators. He wondered whether the Viet Cong raiders who'd slipped back into the jungle after the nighttime assault on Buon Ma had felt the same sense of triumph as these two. *Buon Ma.* The words meant "Sad Ghost." Never had Griswold found them so appropriate.

Edison Markell had apparently forgotten his invitation, for he still strode forward and looped his arm familiarly through that of the promising young summer associate, who would surely get an offer of permanent employment in the fall. Mary Thuy halted, however, and spun around, twirling Markell with her as though they were dance partners. Both of them giggled.

"*Come* with us, Carlton! Won't you?" she pleaded. "Please. For *my* sake, if not for his. Ed says we've got good reason to celebrate." Edison Markell nodded affably.

"*Please,*" she repeated with a smile, when Griswold did not move.

He glared at her and shook his head, but then, when he saw another look of triumph rise to her face, he knew that he would change his mind. Yes, he would accompany them, and yes, he would drink. Long, patiently, and hard. Not to *Warren v. Venturecom Capital Corp. et al.,* but rather to the memory of the two young women he had failed to save. Until Edison Markell, befuddled and dimwitted as always, remembered that he had a wife and child in Hillsborough and sneaked off guiltily to join them, leaving the two of them alone. And then he would drink some more, and make *her* drink with him, for of course she had a weak point and he would find out what it was. And he would make her drink until she was so drunk that he could take her home with him, stupid and senseless, to the only place still dark enough to give him any peace.